FEVE

By
Jacqueline Druga

FEVER
By Jacqueline Druga
Copyright 2017 by Jacqueline Druga

This is a work of fiction. Names, characters, places and incidents are either the product of the author's imagination or are used fictitiously, and any resemblance to any person or persons, living or dead, events or locales is entirely coincidental.

Thank you to Paula, Trisha and Kira for this one. Also, for things you have taught me.

Cover Art by Christian Bentulan
www.coversbychristian.com

ONE - MOMENTS

Everything in life is precious.
Everything.
Nothing is exempt. No positive or negative events, from the simplest of smiles received to the smallest hangnail. If it brings an emotion or feeling it is precious. There's it isn't an instance in life that goes by that doesn't impact our lives in one way or another.

I truly don't believe that mankind forgets or takes for granted these precious moments. We simply graze by them, with little thought or acknowledgment at the time. The hurt, pain, happiness and love, are all too easy to forget after the best of the moment has passed. The memory doesn't disappear, rather the feeling becomes muted. Sometimes it is a blessing, more often it is a curse.

Like childbirth, it is the most excruciating pain a woman can feel, yet if I were asked what it felt like, all I could reply was I knew it hurt. The pain fades. In a way, I wish I could bottle or create a machine that saviors the sensation of every single feeling and every single emotion. When I needed to relive a memory, I would open that bottle or go into that machine. Experience again the happiness, the feeling of first time love. The memories remain, sometimes not as vivid, but those feelings experienced, those emotions that separate us from the animals and make us human, are hard to recapture.

We could generate new feelings, comparable feelings, but they're never the same.

I wished for such a machine or magical bottle, to recapture the way I did on the day I married my husband. I would allow that happiness to drown out the sadness I felt when he left this earth long before his time.

We lived the perfect life. We rarely fought and I loved him. He was my first and only love. A picture perfect family. Sunday dinners, Monday night pizza. From baseball games to shuffling the kids to and from school. Normal was our middle name.

Then Jason got a headache that wouldn't let up.

Three weeks of pain.

What we believed was a sinus infection was actually a form of brain cancer, Glioblastoma. We were told we had at least a year. Within a week of starting treatment and three weeks from his first headache ... Jason was gone. Too soon and too young, he was only thirty-five.

I wanted to crumble and bury myself away from the agony of his death. I didn't have time to even process his illness, much less his death, it was so fast. Instead I got angry. I hid that sadness behind a sea of rage. He left me with three young children, one of which was just a baby, not even a year old.

And the anger built.

I was mad that he didn't keep up the life insurance because he thought he was too young to die. Mad that I was unable to function normally enough to keep my job as a high school teacher.

Enraged because I lost everything, the house, the car ... everything.

I tried so hard to keep going that I lost sight of where I had been. I never grieved him properly, I should have. I needed to and he deserved for me to grieve. He deserved for me to shed tears, to cry that I missed him, run to his grave and talk about my life without him. Because I did miss him, I missed him with every fiber of my being.

I portrayed a pillar of emotional steel for the sake of my children, but I was weak and was bound to cave it. Ignoring everything, burying all emotions until eventually I exploded.

Nothing quite like being in a grocery store eight months after the fact, reaching for a bag of diapers, then suddenly dropping to my knees and sobbing uncontrollably. I frightened the people around me enough the paramedics had to be called.

If it is true that God never gives us more than we can handle, then God misjudged me. I handled Jason's death and the time thereafter, completely wrong.

I had to learn to live life over again.

The wall of strength I projected after his death was a façade; however the strength I gained in the six years since he died was real.

Looking back, I truly believed Jason's death laid the groundwork for how to think, act, feel and process the quick death of a loved one. Although I believed his passing was an emotional preparation for things to come, I also believed there was nothing that could prepare me, or the world for what was ahead.

TWO – FOREWARNING

April 13

"John Ashton never waivers," that's what people said about my father. No matter what the problem, dilemma, if a solution was needed, they went to him. I always saw my father as a pillar. I inherited his unnerving ability to remain calm. The bigger the problem, the calmer my father, yet should someone lose the battery to his remote, he'd have their head.

I knew him to be calm and rational when it came to problems, so when he told me, "Clare, I don't think we should send the kids to school anymore until this thing passes." I knew things were bad.

I just didn't think they were *that* bad, not yet.

"Just as a precaution," my father said. "Let's not send them back."

I tilted my head giving a facial expression that said more than any words.

"I'm serious, Clare. Have you read the news…?"

"I read the news. I just … I don't know. Easter break starts in three days."

"Then no reason for them to go back."

"I'll think about it," I told him, and then I left to retrieve my daughter, Ivy from the grade school. She was the only one who went to Bishop Catholic; my boys went to public school. Eli was in seventh grade and Michael was a junior. They took the bus and hated when I showed up in my old Chevy to get them. But Ivy loved it.

Briefly, I thought about my father's words, then I was sidetracked by Marcia at Starbucks and listening to music in the car.

However, when I pulled into the school lot, I had to check the time. Was I early? Late?

Typically, five minutes before dismissal, the lot was packed. Cars fought for a good spot and those who were lazy parked wherever they wanted. But that wasn't the case on this day.

There was half the number of cars in the lot and despite the nice weather, there wasn't a parent at all waiting by the doors.

Had I missed some sort of memo or emergency email? I stepped from my car and headed to the waiting area. There was an eerie feel to it all. A calm in the air, and I looked around.

I was the only one standing there.

The bell rang and that was my sign that within thirty seconds the doors would open and the kids would come running out, hands flailing, as they headed straight to the arms of awaiting parents.

Parents that stayed by the cars.

One mother made her way to the plaza pick up area and she did so as the doors opened.

Kids came out, but they weren't running and there weren't that many.

"Excuse me?" I called out to the parent. "What's going on?"

Immediately, she covered her mouth, grabbed her son and bolted away without a word.

"Mommy!" Ivy flew to me.

"Hey, sweetie." I leaned down and kissed her, then took her hand to walk to the car.

"Guess what?'

"What?"

"The principal sent an email to you. We don't have school tomorrow."

"Why not?" I asked.

Ivy shrugged. "No one is coming to school. We only had seven kids in my class today."

I paused as I opened the car door. "That's more than half your class. Where were they?"

Ivy snickered as she climbed into her seat. "They were all sick, silly."

I froze.

For a moment, there in the parking lot, I couldn't move. My eyes shifted around. The lack of cars, the parents avoiding each other, half the children in Ivy's class not there.

How did it get that way and so fast? Surely the news would have mentioned if half the students in school weren't showing up.

I shut her door, watched as she buckled into her car seat, then after getting in the car, I pulled out my phone to check my email.

There was one from the school that had come a half hour earlier.

My father was right in his judgment call, but he was behind the eight ball, we should have kept them home earlier.

My entire being shuddered when I read the letter from the principal, *'While not confirmed, we have received reports that several students may have the fever.'*

It was here. It arrived, and if the rumor was true, then every student in that school was exposed, including my daughter.

That email, the empty parking lot.... I didn't need a news station, presidential speech or some virus doctor to tell me. In my gut and in my heart, I knew that day was the beginning ... of the end.

THREE – MILLS RUN

FOUR WEEKS EARLIER - March 23

"Hey, there, Clarabelle," my father gave his typical morning greeting when I walked into the kitchen. "I had this. You didn't need to get up."

He was putting barrettes in my six-year-old daughter, Ivy's hair. She sat at the breakfast table, her school uniform neat and pressed. It was so funny watching him. He wasn't an old man, he was strong and fit, and just looked a little too 'Harley Motorcycle Guy' to be fixing a little girl's hair perfectly.

"The alarm went off, the boys weren't up and …I thought you had to work," I said.

"Boys have another six minutes and no work this morning. Big day."

I thought, *big day*? Was I missing something? Usually anything categorized as "big" in our town was posted all over Mills Run.

I would have preferred to stay in Nashville, but I wasn't making ends meet and Mills Run was a great solution.

When we moved there, my father was struggling on his military pension because of paying an enormous loan on what I called a bad investment. We worked together to pay the bills, my little bit of money I earned from my two part time jobs. Then my father went from being the poorest man in town to the richest.

Which wasn't hard to do in Mills Run.

His bad investment worked out. He predicted most of the mills would close down, and when they started building the new gaming resort and new hotels across the river, he bought an old ferry and refurbished it.

He saw a need, I didn't. I was wrong and John Ashton Ferry was beyond successful.

Mills Run, Ohio wasn't that bad. Actually, it wasn't bad at all. It wasn't a town I grew up in, more so one I visited often. My father was born there and my grandfather never left. A tiny blip on the map located ten miles south of Steubenville on the Ohio River. It gained its name from the steel and coal mills in the area. It wasn't big, not at all. The main part, or downtown, was on the flat surface not far from the river. The houses were on the hillsides that surrounded Mills Run. It had charm, and everything from the bar, diner, overpriced grocer to the library were within walking distance. It was a good thing because when it snowed, nothing shut down, everyone just footed it.

I saw why my father loved it so much. Of course, he got annoyed once the Mills Run Hotel opened back up and all of the sudden, because of the casino resort, Mills Run was a tourist attraction.

Go figure.

My mother even visited often.

She always stayed with us.

My parents never married, which was unheard of when I was a kid, as I grew older, people just assumed my mother and father were divorced. I couldn't recall when they broke up, it was seamless. My father was career navy, accomplishing the rank of Captain. When he was stateside and teaching, I lived with him. Not that I didn't like or love my mother, I did. She was wonderful, but her career was hard to deal with. She was a soap opera actress, the top in her field, winner of many Emmy and 'Tear Queen' awards. She was absolutely stunning and beautiful and the older I got, the harder it was to deal with.

My father let me be me. Jeans and tee shirts. I didn't have to look my best, wear makeup or even do anything more than a ponytail with my hair when I was with him.

Unfortunately, he wasn't the same way with my six-year-old daughter, Ivy. She had to be picture perfect when she went to school; unlike me, Ivy loved it. Of course, she was a sixty-year-old woman trapped in a pint-sized body.

We moved in with my father after Jason's death, when Ivy was only one. My father was the only male father figure she knew.

My sons found their pap "fun."

He hadn't changed much, he was still the stark contradiction to what one would think a career navy man would be.

Fixing my daughter's hair was an example of that contradiction.

He finished fussing with her hair while I retrieved some of that horribly bitter coffee my father made.

Ivy sat straight in her chair smoothing apple butter over a piece of toast.

I leaned against the counter, sipping my coffee, looking at Ivy's hair. It was straight and perfect, not a crimp in it and I swore her dark hair had a spit shine. "I can't believe she lets you get the tangles out."

My father set down the brush. "It's all in preparation. You send her to bed with her hair down. She sleeps, tosses and turns, it ends up everywhere. I put it in a ponytail at night."

"Plus, pappy brushes it with love," Ivy said.

"Hmm, I bet." I gave an upward nod of my chin. "How do you get it so shiny?"

"WD-40."

I nearly spit out my coffee. "I'm sorry ... what? WD-40?"

My father nodded. "WD-40."

"You put a flammable substance on my child's hair?"

He flung out his hand at me. "It's fine. Tiny bit on the brush, shake it, tape it, start with the ends. Plus, it's a great lice repellent."

"All my friends got lice at the beginning of the year," Ivy said nonchalantly. "Not me."

"Oh my God." Shaking my head, I sat down at the table.

"How was work last night?" my father asked.

"Bar was dead." I shrugged. "I made eleven bucks. However... I'm set up for tonight though, that acoustic duo from Liverpool is playing and they bring a huge crowd. I need to start saving for prom."

"Well, I got it if you don't." He opened the newspaper.

"I appreciate the offer. I just want to be able to pay for my son's first prom."

"Be glad it's not a daughter." He winked.

"So, what's the big day?" I asked.

"Special person day at Ivy's school."

"Shit." I started to stand up. "I'll go get ready." The second my butt lifted from the chair, I saw both of them looking at me. "What?"

"I can only take one person, Mommy," Ivy said.

"Oh, Sweetie, Pappy understands. I am sure he ..." I paused, and that was when it dawned on me. Especially when my father just kept reading the paper. "Wait. I'm not the special person going, am I?"

"No, Clare," my father reached up and pulled me back down. "Don't fill the girl with guilt over her decision to take her aging grandfather to a very special event. Lord knows how many more I can attend."

"Aging grandfather my ass, you'll probably outlive me if ..." Then I saw it, it wasn't the headline, but it was large enough for me to see.

'Spain closes border in hopes to feign off Fever'

I leaned over the table trying to read what it said.

"What are you doing?" my father asked.

"I was just looking at the article about Spain. When did they close the borders?"

"They didn't." He shut the paper and folded it. "The headline is misleading. They wanted to. The thing is, borders closed or not, this thing has to run its course, like Ebola, SARS, you name it."

"It's deadly."

He scoffed. "No, it's not."

"Yeah, it is. I read about it."

"On those damn conspiracy sites. I read about it online, too on CNN. No more deadly than the ordinary flu, you just hear about it more." He stood up. "I'm going to get those boys up."

I nodded, sipped my coffee then reached across the table, grabbing the paper.

"Pappy is not done reading, he'll get mad," Ivy said.

"Pappy will deal with it." I took the paper. I would have gone on the internet, but lately we had the worst connection at our house. For some reason, especially during the day and early evening, our high speed was more like dial up.

The story wasn't headlines, nothing about the fever was headlines anymore. Like my father had said, the article was different than the title led me to believe. Everything about the fever seemed sugar coated, every news report and article. Yet, something about borders closing called out to me, probably because deep down I knew better.

FOUR – AN OLD MAN AND HIS DOG

March 28

When I first read about Harry Davis, he was just a little blip in the middle of a big news story, 'The bodies were discovered early that morning by a senior citizen walking his dog.'

That was it.

I was more concerned about the boat with bodies that washed up on the shore of Florida. It was the second time a boat of dead refugees were found. This time, like the previous time, the incident were explained as both boats having gotten lost at sea. The people inside died because of exposure to the elements, and lack of food and water.

Simple row boats packed full of deadly cargo.

Oddly, two survived on the boat Harry Davis found. If they were really out there so long, I don't believe Harry would have found anyone alive.

I didn't think too much about either the boat or Harry Davis until my friend, Trevor brought it up. Trevor was one of those people who found the oddest and scariest stories to read.

In fact, I rarely paid attention to virus or 'outbreak' stories, Trevor did. Amongst other things. He would send me links to things he found on sites like, The Freedom Righter, Truth News or Conservative Science Media.

Usually I'd chuckle or laugh at the ones he sent.

"Trevor," I'd tell him. "There is no giant rat the size of a dog running around New York giving people the plague."

"No, Trevor, we're not getting smashed with that new planet."

"Trev, I highly doubt some massive flu bug is taking over Europe. We'd hear about it."

"We did," he said. "We just didn't pay attention to it."

Why would we? Yet, I had been following the new flu since Trevor brought it to my attention. I followed link after link via text messages.

My ill-informed argument was that 'Flu Season' was September to March, which he counteracted with, "In America."

He had a point. Cold season usually started just before Fall and went through winter until the start of Spring. Autumn didn't start in September everywhere.

When he sent me the link in May about the new flu the previous season, I had dismissed it, until he sent me a fact sheet from the Centers for Disease Control website.

Attention caught. Finally, a real source.

From that moment on, I went on weekly checks to that website. Downloading the data on what was being called a form of H7N2. Technically, it was a strain of bird flu that jumped to cats and then occasionally and often unheard of, jumped to people.

The fact sheet told of cases reported in humans and animals. The Human fatalities were on par with other strains of the flu at one percent.

I wasn't familiar with the geography of the UK, so I didn't know where the locations were of the outbreaks.

It was public knowledge.

What wasn't on the CDC website was a different matter.

The underground papers and conspiracy rags were calling it the Whitby Fever because it started in the small seaside town of Whitby, North Yorkshire, UK.

According to the CDC, roughly ten percent of the fourteen thousand residents came down with the Fever.

According to the Freedom Righter, more than thirty percent came down with the virus and over half of them died.

What also wasn't mentioned was that they had to euthanize four thousand cats and seven hundred dogs.

Slowly it started infecting neighboring villages, one the next month, two the following month. By August, the Whitby Fever had spread to a dozen small villages. Mandatory euthanasia for domestic pets was issued in those towns. Pictures of mass feline and canine graves were posted everywhere on the internet and the conspiracy sites. Orders for body bags, food and camp supplies were also shown.

All the typical conspiracy, end of the world stuff was pretty hot and heavy up until September, then it fizzled when the start of the real cold and flu season hit America.

I still checked constantly, then my interest waned as we moved into the holidays and I forgot about it.

Trevor was back to texting me links to sensational stories.

I was the one who, on Valentine's Day, discovered it was not only back, it had never left and was being lumped into the statistics of the normal flu. Tiny asterisks on the CDC facts sheets next to numbers led to a tiny little footnote which read: "Some of these statistics may include the flu strain H7N2."

What? Like an active ingredient on a product? Like one of those footnote afterthoughts you hear on a commercial about a medication.

'May cause headaches, drowsiness, chills, loss of appetite ...'

Did they think no one would notice? The major news outlets didn't. They stopped mentioning the Fever months earlier.

I was excited, though I don't know why the excitement level kicked in. I had never before been infatuated with a virus story.

Being so consumed, I registered for alerts with the Freedom Righter site, and looked at my list of friends on social media to see who was in the UK for somebody I actually engaged with regularly.

I reached out to him via messenger and casually brought it into a conversation as if it were some sort of taboo subject.

"Yeah, we know about it," Nick said. "The government isn't saying much, but they released an advisory not to travel or plan a holiday over there. That's all we got."

I asked if he'd keep me posted. He said he and his wife were concerned about it, yet it was still north and on the other side of the country at that point, it appeared to not be making any big moves towards them.

I told Trevor about what Nick had told me.

"This is the one," Trevor said. "I really think it could get bad."

It didn't cross my mind what 'this is the one' truly meant. I mean, it was *over there*, right? Like to Nick it was on the other side of the country, I was on the other side of the pond.

Then came Harry Davis.

The Whitby Fever virus started to mutate, it went from being a footnote to being its own page on the CDC website.

It was a concern. While they claimed it was still tough to catch, the mortality rate grew as the days went on. It went from one percent to fifty, and the day I heard Harry Davis' name, they released information from the UK acknowledging the Northern Eastern part of the country was battling an epidemic. Everyone paid attention, it was like the last Ebola outbreak all over again.

Animal rights movements were quick to travel to the UK and Denmark, both countries issuing warning that if domestic pets showed any signs of ailment to call their local animal control or rescue center and surrender the pet.

To me it was scary.

So was Harry Davis.

Not the man, Harry Davis, I never met him. So, I can't say if he was scary, his situation was. I feared what would come next.

It was a pretty big news story, the second refuge ship to wash ashore in two weeks. How the latest was found by a man walking his dog.

They said his name was Harry Davis. I envisioned this old man walking his dog on the beach, coming across body after body on the beach. A map of carnage that led him to the over turned boat. Actually, my imagination wasn't that great, I envisioned more so from the story told in the Freedom Righter.

I felt bad for the refugees, all they wanted was to taste the freedom of America and they found heartache and death.

I didn't connect the dots, in fact I didn't think there was even a connection to the refugees until Trevor said, "What if....?"

Nah.

Then we looked.

Sure enough, there were cases of Whitby Fever, or ERDS, as the World Health Organization called it in Cuba. Havana had over a hundred cases.

What if these people had it? What if they brought it to our shores?

Immediately, I thought of Harry Davis and like any good modern woman, I looked him up on social media.

The nice thing about having a famous mother is the amount of people that seek you out after attending an event with her. Harry and I had forty mutual friends and he accepted my request right away.

Oddly enough, Harry messaged me.

"You related to Melinda Ashton?" he asked. "You look just like her."

"She's my mother," I replied.

"What do you know. You look like sisters."

I hated that comment. I always wondered if they were saying her facial upkeep was working, or I just looked old.

I didn't exchange many more messages, but like a big creeper I watched his time line.

Harry updated frequently, stating he would do so because he wanted his daughter to follow his journey.

He left Key Largo, rented out the house he owned there, and headed for his yearly pilgrimage north in his RV to see his daughter.

That was March twenty-fifth. The day after he found the bodies.

March twenty-six, he posted that he had to stop at a vet in Florence, South Carolina because his dog was sick.

On March twenty-seventh, Harry said the dog wasn't better and that he was tired and making a pit stop for the night somewhere in Virginia.

The refugees, the sick dog... Harry unwell.

My mind raced.

In a strange occurrence, Harry didn't post at all the next day.

I checked using my phone and planned on checking again when I got to my other job at the Quick Med in town. The connection was so much better there.

Not that I knew anything about medical stuff, but I got the job because I was willing to work as a receptionist one day a week, and the doctor who ran it, frequented my other job at the bar.

We were always busy at Quick Med, even more so on the weekends.

My father had a special senior citizen tour cruise on his ferry that had him out of the house longer and my oldest, Michael was in charge of Eli and Ivy. I had no problem with that. Michael was the most responsible sixteen year old I knew.

He didn't get lost on his phone or computer. I never had to worry about him playing video games and not paying attention, that wasn't Michael. He was mature, loved to read and was working on a puzzle when I grabbed my purse to leave.

"Pap will be back by four," I said. "Where's Ivy?"

"In her room. She's fine," Michael said. His curly brown hair needed cut I noted as it danced in his eyes.

"Eli." I walked to the couch. I knew he was there, I could see the back of my son's head. "Eli." I paused, then said his name louder. "Eli!"

"What. Aw you made me lose." He lowered his tablet for a moment then lifted it again.

"Sorry. Anyhow, listen to Michael, he's in charge."

No response.

"Did you hear me?"

"Okay."

I rubbed his head and walked to the door.

"Mom," Michael called me. "Did you read this?"

I paused. "I don't need to read, Michael. I know what a delayed entry program is."

"Pap says …"

"Pap isn't your father."

"The recruiter needs your signature so he can …"

"The recruiter needs to make his quota." I lifted my keys from my purse and I realized I had been cutting him off. "I'm sorry. We'll talk about this later, okay? I promise. You just dumped it on me yesterday."

Michael was congenial, he nodded.

"Thank you for watching them. Call me if you need me." I opened the door and reached for my phone to see the time, hoping I could walk to Quick Med. As soon as I saw that I could, my phone rang.

Trevor?

He never called. He always sent a text.

"Hey," I answered as I started to walk. "What's wrong?"

"Did you see the news?" Trevor asked.

"No. What happened?"

"They just confirmed that second boat of refugees had Whitby Fever."

I stopped walking as if I couldn't process the information and move at the same time. "Are you shitting me?"

"No, I shit you not."

I started walking again.

"There's more. They tracked down Harry because he found the boat, right? Both him and his dog are dead."

"Oh, my God!"

"They didn't say if it was the fever, they're saying more than likely not, but get this, they shut down that vet clinic in South Carolina as a precaution."

I breathed deeply and continued walking. "Send me some links, I'll look at work when I can get a good connection." I hung up with Trevor and picked up the pace.

Suddenly, my enthusiasm to learn more about the Whitby Fever wasn't out of fascination. It had turned into a realistic fear.

The Whitby Fever was no longer far away, across the pond infected small shore towns. It was no longer on an island south of Florida. It was on American soil. If Harry Davis' last check post was correct, the fever didn't just land in the United States, it made it all the way to Virginia.

FIVE – NEEDLESS WORRY

The blast of the twelve o'clock fog horn on my father's ferry told me I was on time for my clinic shift. He always gave a two horn tug when he left or passed Mills Run at noon. I relieved Maryanne whom probably would have liked to be out the door at noon, I tried, I really did. It was better when I relieved her at one, at least then I was usually early.

The Quick Med was a new ala cart style, one stop and go, low price convenience store of all your non-life threatening health needs. It didn't start with just one or two, a whole slew of them opened up in the tri-state area. Mills Run got a Quick Med when the casino opened up and they transformed the old Pizza Hut building. I swore sometimes I still smelled pizza.

It was pretty popular among the locals and on weekends we treated a lot of hangovers from young people visiting the resort. It was a strange operation, but well thought out. They didn't have a one price fits all when it came to examinations and treatments. You paid according to what you received and for the residents of Mills Run, it was the affordable alternative.

The commercial was pretty funny. Like a used car salesman, Dr. Daljit Singh, the owner of all the clinics, walked through a Quick Med, "Are you tired of over-paying just because you have a splinter ….?"

He was right. I know I related. Once, before the Quick Med, I had to take Eli to a medical express on a Sunday. We walked in, told the symptoms, the doctor looked in his ear and diagnosed infection, then wrote a prescription. We were there an entire ten minutes from entrance to exit … a hundred and fifty dollars.

That same scenario at Quick Med was considered a simple exam and was only twenty-five dollars.

The clinic made money off of add ons. Consultations, different types of sutures, tie sling versus Velcro. It was crazy, yet it worked and I enjoyed my Saturday shift there.

Maryanne ran out before I even sat in the chair, I could hear Dr. Singh on the phone as he walked back and forth. He used one of those annoying ear pieces that made it look like he talked to himself.

It was the younger, Dr. Singh, the son. His name was Samir, we called him Sam. He was born in India and went back and forth between there and America. Not a tall man, Sam had a round face that spread wider when he smiled and a healthy build. He was youthful, fun and a ball of energy, unlike his father who was stern and miserable. I was grateful that Sam came to the Quick Med three times a week instead of his father. The rest of the time we had a Nurse Practioner. Sam's biggest downfall was he charged everyone the lowest rate. Even if he was in there for an hour. Then we, the staff heard about it from his father.

"Oh, Clare, it's you," Sam said coming into the reception area.

"Um, yeah, it's Saturday. Who else would be here?" I sat behind the counter.

"Your father."

"What?" I laughed. "Why would my father be here?'

"He said he was getting you to drive the Miss Daisies and he would work for you."

"What are you talking about?"

"The senior citizen casino junket. Get it driving Miss ...?"

"Oh, my God, I get it. Stay out of the eighties, or whenever that movie came out. I only operate the Ferry if needed for events on Sundays. Besides, my father has no idea what to do."

"Do you?" Sam smiled widely and then laughed hard at his own joke.

"Yeah, yeah, keep up the bad jokes at my expense and I won't give you a double when you come in my bar."

He quickly stopped laughing. "I'm going to be in the office. Japanese Baseball is starting."

"Hey ... Sam?" I called to him before he went too far. "What do you know about the Whitby Fever? "

"The what?"

"The flu bug in Europe."

"Oh." He nodded slowly. "More than you."

"I doubt that."

"You called it Whitby Fever, it is called ERDS. European Respiratory Distress Syndrome."

"Yeah, but no one really gets to that point," I said. "They die from the fever. The dogs and cats are spreading it."

"Other than occasional kennel cough, dogs don't spread illness to people."

"Wrong. H7N2 is passed on to humans from pets."

Sam rubbed his head. "Miss know it all, if you know so much, why do you quiz me?"

"Because I was wondering if you got any alerts. I mean, with Harry dying?"

"Who?"

"Harry Davis. He died."

"I am very sorry, did he die of ERDS?" Sam asked.

"No one knows. I think he did."

"I am very sorry for the loss of your friend. I assure you, there is no ERDS in Mills Run.."

"Oh he's not from Mills Run. I don't really know him. He was the guy a few days ago that found the body of the dead refugees."

Sam walked away.

"Sam. Seriously, those in the boat, the dead refugees, they died of Whitby Fever, that was confirmed."

He stopped walking and looked at me. I saw the moment of alarm hit his face. "Really?" he asked.

"Yes. Now Harry is dead, I thought maybe you may have gotten an alert."

Sam shook his head. "No. So I'm going to say, if this was all that much to worry about it, I would have gotten something. We didn't. So, no worries, but I will look into the boat story."

"Thanks." I swiveled my chair to the computer.

"Clare, today ... up sell."

I gave him a thumbs up in acknowledgement of his request for me to try to convince people to add more services, then I navigated to a web browser.

"Stay off the net. We do not pay you to post kitten pictures on social media."

"I never post kitten pictures," I said as I continued my task. I wasn't dismissing what he said, I just wasn't going on Social Media. I was looking for news about Harry and the fever. Since that was all medical stuff, I could vaguely say it was work related, and research on the internet guilt-free. Our connection at the Quick Med was almost as good as the bar and I was going to take advantage of a speedy search.

<><><><>

The Quick Med was near the river and when I left at six o'clock I saw my father walking up the dock. For some reason I thought he would have been back sooner. Then I remembered he had done a casino sponsored senior citizen junket. This meant he didn't just leave Mills Run, he had to go south past Sistersville and start his pickups at ten, getting his ferry which was full of people to the casino by 12:30, and picking them back up four hours later. He had to go back down river making it a long run. He looked tired. I waited for him so we could walk home together.

"Hey, there, Clarabelle. How was the clinic? When I docked, I thought you were closed." He kissed me on the cheek.

"That's why I don't drive. If there's no car, people think we're closed. It was good. I worked with Samir today. He's fun. How was the junket?"

"You know how they go. Rowdy, happy, drinking women on the way there. Miserable people on the way home because they lost."

"Sucks. Michael had a stress-free day with Eli and Ivy."

"Yeah, I know, he sent me a text. He has a date tonight and asked if he could use the car."

"You think he's okay?" I asked. "He just got his license.'

"He's fine. Most responsible kid I know. Speaking of responsible…"

"Uh, oh, what did I do?"

"Nothing. Wanted to ask you before we hit the hill. Feel like taking the seven, eight and nine tonight?"

"What happened to Bill?" I asked.

"He called off sick."

"Oh, no, he doesn't have Whitby Fever, does he?"

"What?" My dad laughed.

"The fever? European Flu? ERDS?"

"No," he said, laughing harder. "He has gout."

"I have no idea what that really is. He wasn't at the Quick Med."

"I got news for you, not everyone goes there," he said. "So, will you? I just want to relax and I promised Ivy we'd watch that John Wayne movie tonight."

"Um, can I go to Pepper's Mill?"

"Were you supposed to work there tonight?"

"No, I want to use the internet. Maybe have a drink."

My father held up a finger. "Just one. You know how river patrol has been. I don't need you getting a BUI."

"Just one, I promise."

"That's fine. Thanks for taking the shift." He kissed me again. "See you in a bit. Josh should relieve you after you get back from the nine."

My father and I parted ways. He made his way toward the hill and our home. I veered towards town to go to Pepper's Mill, the place I tended bar a couple days a week.

I didn't mind filling in for my father. I enjoyed it when the weather was nice. My father taught me how to operate the ferry before he launched it. Then I studied and it took three tries passing the safety course to get my boating card. Once I had it, I was the fill-in operator at least once a week.

I knew the bar wouldn't be crowded yet. It was early on a Saturday evening.

Sure enough, Doc Samir was in there seated at his usual spot, last stool on the left.

Patch was tending bar. Patch wasn't his real name, rather a nickname Gordon Pepper, the owner, had given to him because he couldn't pronounce his last name.

Patch had been in Mills Run for as long as I could remember. I remember meeting him when I'd visit my grandfather. I never spoke to him much. He was a few years older than me, but honestly looked younger. Patch, or rather Jael Pacheco, met Gordon outside of Pittsburgh when he was eighteen. Patch was broken down on the side of the road on the parkway and Gordon stopped to help. The car was old, unable to be repaired, and Jael was just heading south from New York. He was trying to go somewhere following the death of his mother, the only family member he had. He was young, alone and scared, and Gordon took a liking to him.

He offered Jael a job to make some money and save for his trip. Jael never left Mills Run. Despite being in Mills Run since he was eighteen, he never quite developed the native look. He stood out like a sore thumb, in a good way. Jael was probably the best-looking guy in town. He was built well without going to a gym, he had a dark Latino look, with stylishly cut hair, daring sideburns, with a killer perfect white smile. He said he got the hair, smile and clothes from Steubenville. I didn't believe that because I didn't think Steubenville was a fashion town.

"Look who it is. Aren't you going home?" Sam asked.

"No, I have to take a ferry Shift."

"You're going to drink and boat?'

"One." I said. "And who are you to talk? You have a bottle in your bottom drawer at the clinic."

"You two ..." Jael placed a glass before me. "Double and coke?"

"No, just a single and coke. I have the ferry. Bill's sick and no ..." I looked at Sam. "He doesn't have the fever."

"Didn't think he would." Sam sipped his drink.

"I hear that's pretty bad," Jael said.

"See, I did, too. Hey, do you have your tablet?"

"Yes, why?" he asked hesitantly.

"Can borrow it? I have to go online."

He finished making my drink, then walked away to grab it. He handed it to me. "Make sure you log me out, please. Don't post any 'Clare is the best' comments on my account please, my girlfriend will get mad."

"You mean this week's girlfriend will be mad? Last week's didn't care."

He grumbled a 'hmm' as he handed me the tablet.

"Thanks," I said. Taking the tablet and my drink, I went to a booth, sat down and propped the tablet on its case. As soon as I cleared his screen saver, I saw that he had been on his favorite dating site. I guessed this week's girlfriend was on her way out. I didn't understand why he needed a dating site, all he had to do was post he was single.

I closed out that site and went to social media. He was logged in. Just as I was about to sign him out, I took a sip of my drink, looked over at Patch and then, giggling I posted, 'Clare came to visit, love when she stops by'. I posted, logged out, then signed into mine. I was just about to comment something witty to that post when I noticed I had three missed video calls from Nick.

I hadn't heard from Nick in days.

I realized it was late on his side of the world, yet the last missed video call was only twenty-minutes earlier. So, I reached out.

The call was answered right away and I could see Nick's arm, then he sat in the frame.

"Hey, Nick, what's going on? I missed your call."

He looked over his shoulder. I could hear the television in the background, then he returned his attention to me. He looked frazzled.

"Did I wake you?" I asked.

"It's here," he said softly.

"What is?"

"The Whitby Fever. You were asking about it. I said it was no worries. It's here."

"In the UK, I know."

"No." He shook his head. "Here. In Buckley, Wales... London. It started two days ago in Sheffield when the vet at an animal hospital came down with it. All the animals he saw that day, died within a day. Exactly like over there."

"Wait, that didn't happen here?"

Nick nodded. "In North Carolina or South. I don't remember.

"Hold on." I grabbed my phone and immediately searched. I used words like Vet, ERD, fever, clinic and died. Nothing came up. I also looked up the outbreak in the UK. "Nick, I can't find anything. Can you send me a link?"

"Hold on." Nick must have minimized his screen, I could hear the tap of his fingers, then he returned. "Sent you the news site."

The link popped up in a message and I clicked on it. "Holy shit."

"What?"

"This site is unavailable in your country."

"I've sent you links to that site many times."

"Well, I can't get there today."

"You must be on information lock down. Three of my posts disappeared today. I'll do some screen shots straight away and send them to you."

"Thank you," I said. "What are they saying?"

"Not much about how it spreads. It either was already in the population, or there was a way that it passed rapidly. It has a very short incubation. They say the worst carriers are cats and dogs. There's a mandatory surrender. Clare ... I had to take my dog in yesterday." His voice cracked. "He was a part of my family for twelve years." He took a moment to compose himself.

"How bad is it where you live?"

"Bad. It happened so fast. Three days ago, I was at the market, today, there's only emergency personnel on the streets. They're saying to stay inside. I heard London is in chaos. There's no cure, no treatment. It hits fast and it kills fast. The little girl next door died. I could hear her mother screaming."

My hand shot to my mouth and my heart dropped to my stomach. It made me sick. How could something spread so fast without anyone knowing about it?

"I'll get on those screen shots. When we talked about it, I thought you were crazy. It was just a virus." He chuckled emotionally.

"How are you feeling, Nick?"

"Me? I'm fine for now. Doubt I will be for long." He sniffed. "My wife is sick with it."

"Oh, Nick. I am so sorry."

He shook his head. "I'll try to stay in contact. I'll send you that info. That way you can be informed and perhaps find a way to prepare for when it hits your town."

"Maybe it won't. Maybe we'll get lucky."

"No. It's already in America. It's just a matter of time." Nick turned his head quickly, I could hear the call of his name from the background. A long drawn out call. He faced me again. "I have to go."

Connection over.

I sat back in the booth, staring at the tablet, trying to absorb all that he told me. It just didn't seem real to me. Instead of sipping, I downed my drink, perhaps my way of numbing the painful dose of truth I had just received, a truth I didn't want to acknowledge, or face.

SIX – NORMAL LIFE

March 29

There was nothing on the news. Absolutely nothing. I checked, nothing about the UK or the veterinary clinics. The CDC hadn't updated the fact sheets on ERDS and it looked like all was well. In the meantime, I read the screen shots Nick sent me. Across the ocean, all was not well.

It wasn't just the UK, there were other countries in Europe reporting it. I had Trevor look for information on the vet. He found a small mention in an obscure local paper in South Carolina.

Nothing stated made it seem epidemic. Yet, I was obsessed. Every second I had, I was flipping through channels on the television, not only using my data on my phone, something I never did, but making it a hot spot and connecting it to my laptop outside.

My text to Trevor read, 'get back to me', I hit send, placing my phone on my bed, then reaching for the remote.

"Mommy?" Ivy called my name.

"Yes, sweetie?"

She walked up to me and sighed. "Pappy says you have to get downstairs."

"I will in a minute."

"He said to tell you …. now."

"I will in a minute. It's top of the hour, I just want to catch the headlines."

Ivy darted a kiss to my cheek. "Okay, I'll tell him."

"That was sweet." I touched my cheek.

"You'll need that to hold on to when he comes up and yells at you."

"He's not going to yell. I'll be right down." After she left, I aimed the remote at the television. I knew the channel numbers for the big three networks and the 24/7 local news access. My new found 'flipping channel' skill allowed me to skim the headlines.

'The National Centers of the arts has announced its annual ....'

Flip.

'FAA says pilot error was to blame in the fatal crash of Flight 247. The plane crashed a hundred miles short of its Orlando destination last December killing all 168 on board ...'

Flip

'The Governor of Virginia has declared a state of emergency for Cape Charles...'

Yes, I thought, this is it.

'.... After a series of storms left the area flooded ...'

Flip.

'A Pennsylvania man, Calvin Stewart, has been sentenced to twenty-five years on eight counts of vehicular homicide and driving under the influence. At sentencing Friday, families of the victims pleaded with the court for a life sentence. One family member, however, stated that she forgave him, knew he was remorseful and oddly, asked the court for leniency, stating Stewart would carry the burden the rest of his life and that was punishment enough. Her testimony must have had some weight considering the sentence. Faye Wills lost her husband and two children in that fatal pile ..."

"Clare."

Engrossed in the local story, I jumped when my father called my name and shut off the TV.

"What are you doing?" he asked.

"I was watching the news. There's nothing about the virus on there at all."

"Clare, for God sakes, stop this. Okay? There's nothing on there because there is nothing to report."

"That's not true," I argued.

"People will get like you, so they aren't letting the information out. They don't want to scare people. If it's here …"

"It is."

He huffed out in frustration. "If it is, then it stops here. We have amazing medical research. The buck stops here. It will end before it starts. Trust me. Now … downstairs."

"Dad…."

"Really, Clare? Now." He walked out.

Like a scolded child, I grabbed my phone, pouting and followed. It was Sunday afternoon, the one day of the week every single one of us was home. So, why did the Army Recruiter pick a Sunday to come to our house? Didn't he have a life? Anything better to do? Was his quota that bad? Like a car salesman trying to hit his mark before the month was over. It sounded mean, I knew it, but he was really persistent.

It irritated me. Now I had to give up my Sunday to talk to him.

The recruiter was in full uniform, he extended his hand to me when I walked into the living room.

"Mom, this is Sergeant Stockard," Michael introduced us.

"Ma'am."

"Sergeant." I folded my arms closed in a guarded manner.

"I've been talking to your father and Michael," Stockard said. "About the split entry program. Now …"

"I know what the split entry program is," I cut him off. "It's where he gives up the summer between his junior and senior year to be shaped, shifted and beaten in basic training. Then he finishes school and goes back. So, yes, I know."

"Clare," my father said my name sternly. "Why are you so hostile about this?"

"Why aren't you?" I asked, then looked at the sergeant. "I have no problem whatsoever with my child serving his country. None. When he's an adult. My father served his whole life. But my father also waited until he was out of high school."

"Mom, this is something I want to do," Michael said.

"How do you know?" I asked. "Because he told you?" I pointed to the recruiter. "You're sixteen years old."

"I'll be seventeen next month."

"Right now you're sixteen. When I was sixteen I wanted to be a master chef and right now I can't fry an egg to save my life. Things change. I sign that paper, giving permission, that cannot change. You are stuck. They did this to the nuns, you know."

My father laughed loudly. "What the hell are you talking about?"

"Grandma used to tell me," I said. "Back in the day, they'd talk to Catholic girls, convince them when they were young that's what they wanted. The mothers and fathers, signing away their girl to the church before they even knew what they were doing. Same thing. Different job."

"What's a nun?" Ivy asked.

"Something that doesn't exist in America anymore because they abused the recruiting practices."

"Ma'am," Stockard smiled politely to me. "I understand your apprehension. I have a teenage boy myself. I'm here to talk. Not to rush."

"Really?" I asked. "Because this was just thrown at me the other day. Now you're here, in my house, on our family day, wanting to talk to me about my son spending his last summer …."

My words trailed off. I heard myself say, 'Last Summer' and for some reason it had a very eerie effect on me. I wanted to say, 'Last Summer as a kid', but the words didn't emerge. What if it was the last summer?

"Clare," my father snapped me out of it. "What's wrong with you?"

"Huh?" I looked at my father. "I lost my train of thought. I was saying ..." I stopped when my phone vibrated and I heard the different ring. I pulled it out and looked. A video call from Nick. "I'll be back." I slid the 'answer' button over and headed to the door.

"Why are you leaving?" my father asked.

"I have to take it, it's a video call and we don't have reception inside." I walked outside to the edge of the property to get the best reception I could. When I saw Nick, I knew something was wrong. He looked bad, really bad.

"Clare," he said my name and coughed.

No one believed me about the virus, if they could only see and hear Nick. When that thought hit me, I swiped away for a split second, opened the app to record my screen and returned to Nick.

"I'm sorry," I said. "I have to record this. People need to know."

"I have it."

I closed my eyes tightly. "No."

"Yes. I went to the government set up to get me and Chrissie tablets. They're giving relief medication. There is no cure. I have no energy. Every part of my body hurts. My fever ... it's forty."

He was talking Celsius, and I knew that was high. "Nick, get some rest, go to bed, don't worry about ..."

"No." He shook his head. The video distorted some, and was choppy due to the connection. "So you know. It starts with a nosebleed. Then a headache and the fever comes straight away. Everything is bleeding even my gums." He leaned closer to the camera, pulled his bottom lip and exposed his blood tainted teeth. "My ears." Nick turned to show his ear. "My ears are bleeding. What the hell....?"

Done.

End of transmission.

Immediately I tried to reconnect, I couldn't connect. I was instantly sick to my stomach. Why didn't the public know about this? I never would have believed that the government would conceal something so vital. I had to do something. Looking down at my phone, I saw the screen record app was still running. I stopped it and hit 'yes' to save the file.

"Clare?"

I looked back to the house. My father was on the porch.

"You coming back in? Please."

"Yes." I nodded, slipped my phone back in my pocket and walked toward the house.

I knew my mind would be elsewhere while the recruiter tried to convince me to sign away my son. Thoughts of Nick, his wife and all they were going through flickered in the back of my mind. Instantly, I clung to my father's words that the 'buck stopped here', that the outbreak would end before it conquered America. I prayed he was right, because if he wasn't, it didn't matter what the recruiter said or if I signed anything. If what happened in the UK happened in America, there wouldn't be a split entry for Michael to join. There wouldn't be much of anything at all, because from what I learned, that virus only took. It took and took until nothing was left.

SEVEN – STEP BACK

April 4

Never try to be a hero.

I don't mean that if someone is on trouble, stand by the sidelines and watch. Rather, don't put yourself out there. I learned the hard way.

I was appalled that my friend Nick was dying and many others like him, somehow we in the US were protected from such information.

Information, was to me, half the battle. You can't be prepared if you don't know.

That night I took my screen shot of Nick's notes, the video and anything else I had and drove to WTOV 9 in Steubenville. I showed the security guard who was blown away.

"Oh, man," he said, "People have to know this."

"They do, right?"

Immediately he called upstairs and a producer came down, he was followed by Dan Stein. I was a bit nervous, however they both were excited about what I had. They were like, "This is astonishing, how are we not aware of this?"

They then called WPXI in Pittsburgh and by the eleven o'clock news, the story broke.

Strong words were used.

"Travesty!"

"Outrage"

"Fucking government!"

In the first two days, I was interviewed left and right, Mills Run was famous, Gordon, who owned the bar was thrilled. My father added extra ferry runs.

The story just didn't break, it was an expose. The CDC admitted, 'Yes, we have cases, it's under control.'

Then I went from hero to hash tag loser, amongst the many things I was called. The story came to surface on Sunday night and by Tuesday the CDC, WHO and the FBI was discrediting the story. They began interviewing people that said they had the fever and beat it.

They showed pictures and videos of every day normal life in the UK, Spain, Germany. It didn't help that I was the daughter of Malinda Ashton.

Suddenly I was an attention seeker, wanting my fifteen minutes of fame because my mother had just done a made-for-TV movie about a virus. They brought up the time I claimed, while my mother was in an interview, that my dog had five legs. I had duct taped a stuffed toy leg to him. I was only nine for crying out loud.

Then there was poor Nick and his wife.

To them, he wasn't dead. They were reporting that he was a notorious internet hoaxer and that this wasn't the first time he tried to pull a 'War of the Worlds' type rouse.

It wasn't right. It wasn't. Nick had died, I knew it and to desecrate his memory to keep things a secret was just sad.

There were so many people at the bar when I worked, that I started price gouging. Not under Gordon's orders, but rather by how upset they made me.

Jael tried to defend me, but he was a product of ridicule so I made him stop.

"You know, Clare, my girlfriend thinks that you are afraid to admit you made it up," Jael said.

"Oh, fuck your girlfriend."

Which was not a typical response from me.

I knew what I knew, and I felt it was real. I really did. I was outnumbered.

My father was indifferent, "I believe you believe it," sort of thing.

I think Dr. Singh actually believed me. He even told me, "Sometimes Clare, it's best to swallow our pride for what is good for everyone else."

I didn't understand quite what that meant so I gave him a free double, courtesy of my overcharging Fox News.

Trevor sent me texts to see how I was doing. I didn't understand why it wouldn't die down or stop.

It was a hellish three days, it took everything I had to keep it together for myself and my kids. I was strong, too.

Until Thursday night when the bar was packed, someone laughed and said, "Oh look Clare, your mom is on Celebrity Gossip Zone."

Great, I thought, *my own mother will now publicly discredit me.* While washing glasses, I turned to watch the television.

"Malinda," the reporter called to her and my mother stopped walking. "What do you think of your daughter's apocalypse virus hoax?"

"What do I think? I think other than a badly played dog prank by a little girl, my daughter has had plenty of opportunities to seek fame. Why hasn't she before? She's not doing it for attention."

"So, you believe her?"

"Absolutely. Something is going on. Really we should be looking further into this."

"How do you explain the videos of London, the CDC have of people that beat the fever?"

My mother laughed. "Considering what I do for a living, I can explain anything I see on television as the work of great actors and a mighty good production budget. I watched London blow up once in a movie. Did it really happen? No, now excuse me."

She got in her car, someone suggested it was a ploy to promote her new TV Movie, to which my mother told them, "Oh, fuck off." Before shutting the car door and ignoring the rest of the questions.

It was earlier in the day her time, and she put herself out there.

I dropped a glass that I was washing and I emotionally folded, my mother believed me. Then like a five year old child, I ran to the back and called her, sobbing, "Mommy, what am I gonna do?'

"It'll be fine. The world will see. In the meantime, I will be there Sunday. Okay? We'll sort through this."

It wasn't something I told my father, I figured he'd deal with it when my mother showed up, that was my focus. Forgetting what people said, forging forward and waiting until the master of paparazzi showed up to save the day.

I was thrown a little, even felt foolish when I got a social media message from Nick.

"Sorry to drag you into this."

That was all it said.

Last I saw, Nick was bleeding out his ears. I immediately tried to video chat, he didn't answer. Was this an elaborate hoax on his part? No, it couldn't have been because it didn't start with Nick. Maybe he just ran with it. He didn't however, make Harry die or Harry's dog.

'It's part of the cover up," Trevor said in a text. "Don't doubt yourself."

I'd hang onto those words until my mother arrived.

That Saturday my father wasn't feeling well due to a migraine and he asked if I would take the first shift, three trips before I worked at Quick Med. There was a new guy starting, he had his boating safety card and just needed more training on backing up and moving forward.

While I wasn't one for patience in training, I agreed so my father could rest.

The kids were all sleeping when I left. Poor things were caught up in my drama and they didn't know whether to stick out their necks, or bury their heads.

It was chilly out, I sent a text to Dr. Singh telling him I would be a few minutes late and to ask Maryanne not to bitch. I wore my gray hoodie and wind breaker, carrying my silver insulated coffee cup as I walked to the shore.

The river was going to be cold.

I unlocked the ticket booth and flipped on the light, then opened the gate to the Ferry, I didn't see any signs of the new guy, I'd wait for him to untie it. I had several minutes and I had to get the complimentary coffee brewing in the big machine, but when I walked in, the lights were on and I could smell the coffee.

Must be the new guy.

It wasn't. It was Connie, our ticket booth woman.

"Thank you for doing this," I told her.

"Sure thing. Where's John?"

"Oh, my father's sick." I poured coffee into my mug.

"Not that fever thing is it?"

"Is that a dig?" I looked over the rim of my cup.

"No, seriously. I believe you."

I nodded. "No, it's a migraine."

"Oh, good." She grabbed her own cup and started to walk. "I'm heading to the booth. I want to get my space heater going."

"Radio me when the new guys gets here," I said.

"Oh, he's here. Can't you smell him?"

"He's here?" I asked. "What? Does he stink? Great I have to be in the wheelhouse ..."

"Cologne."

"Swell. Where is he?"

She pointed up.

"He's in the wheelhouse? Oh, my God, the nerve. Thanks." New people never took the wheelhouse, ever, I was captain and he should have waited for me below.

I radioed to Blaine who worked the engine room, then I made my way up to the wheelhouse.

I was proud of my father's ferry.

When he purchased it, I didn't see his vision. An old 1979 passenger ferry, he put in new engines, new propulsions, fuel tanks and water storage. Aside from giving her a facelift on the outside, he removed the all-row style seating and added more of a lounge feel on the upper and main decks. He redid the six berths and two staterooms. The ferry was beautiful. A part of me suspected that my mother helped him out, I just couldn't see my father affording it all on his own.

He even put in a bar, which was only used when the ferry was rented out. That happened quite a bit during the summer, overnight cruises.

I made it up to the wheelhouse and before I walked in I caught the scent of cologne. I recognized it and opened the door. Sure enough, wearing a skipper hat and standing at the helm was Jael.

"What in the world are you doing here?" I asked.

"I am the new captain."

"Yeah, well, I'm the captain right now. You're wearing my cap."

"Sorry." He took it off and handed it to me.

"How long have you known you were going to work for us?"

"About two weeks. Just after your father booked the bachelorette party for the governor's daughter."

"I didn't even know you knew how to operate a ferry."

"I didn't." he shrugged. "You father taught me."

"If you didn't know anything about ferries, then why did my father…" It hit me, I knew why. "My father hired you because you look like a male stripper."

"Whatever it takes. It pays well."

"How well?" I asked.

"Better than Pepper's."

"Ha," I laughed in sarcasm. "Everything pays better than Peppers. What is he paying you?"

"I'm not allowed to tell."

"Jael, I won't get mad. I don't get paid," I said.

"You don't."

"No. My father doesn't pay me."

"That's terrible, still, I promised your father I wouldn't say."

"Fine. So, he hired you two weeks ago as eye candy and you didn't say anything. Why didn't you tell me?"

"He said not to."

"Why do you listen to my father?" I asked.

"Everyone does."

"Okay, did he at least teach you?"

"Oh, John's been a great teacher. I have been learning since he hired me. Still struggle when I back up into the dock, Blaine has to direct me. But I'm good at steering …. I know all the equipment. I can press autopilot when I need to use the bathroom. And …I know how to blow the horn."

"Yeah, just don't…"

Jael pressed the horn button.

"Don't blow the horn."

"Sorry."

I held out my hand. "Boater safety card please."

"Seriously?"

"Yeah, I am very serious. State of Ohio requires every boat operator to pass the state boater safety course and carry the card."

Jael reached into his back pocket, opened his wallet and handed me the card.

"Wait a second," I said. "This is dated almost a week ago. It takes a good week to finish the course."

"It was taken on line."

"Still. It took me three tries to pass the test and I knew my stuff."

"Your father took it for me."

I gasped in shock. "He cheated?"

Jael shrugged. "He wanted me to work for him."

I liked Jael, I really did, but it was just unfair that my father hired him when there were other people in town, who knew more, and were far more qualified for the job. It was just so sexist that my father gave him a job because of the way he looked. My father and I would have words.

"Alright," I said. "Did he teach you how to fire things up with Blaine?"

Jael nodded.

"Do you know your cabin checks and how to pull her out.?"

"Yes, I did the Pittsburgh run with him last week, he's been letting me man the boat."

"I'll double check with Blaine on that. Ok, so ..." I felt the buzz in my back pocket and I pulled out my phone. It was a text without a name, from a number I didn't know. It wasn't unusual, since the news broke and I was considered a hoaxer, everyone seemed to have my number. I was getting ready to dismiss it, then I read it.

'You don't know me. I am Dr. Daryl Lewis formally of the CDC. I am sorry for all that you are going through. Just know, for your sanity, the virus is real. In a short time, you will not look like a liar anymore. Please don't respond back, I will not write again.'

That simple message took the air out of me.

Even though I hated being called a prankster, the thought of the virus being real was worse.

"Clare?" Jael called my name. "You okay?"

I cleared my throat. "Yeah." I handed him the cap. "Start the engines. I'll go do the checks." Phone in hand, I turned. Outside the wheelhouse, I read it once more. Not only did the breeze chill the air, that mysterious text from a Dr. Lewis sent an ominous shiver up my spine.

<><><><>

Jael docked the ferry just fine and blew the noon horn. I left him in Blaine's hands and quickly disembarked. I saw my father making his way, in a hurried pass, I darted a kiss to his cheek, told him I hoped he felt better and made my way as fast as I could to the Quick Med.

Surprising me was my son Eli, sitting right out front holding a Pasty's Place takeout bag.

"Aw," I said. "For me?"

"Pap said you'd be hungry."

"I am. You guys are so sweet." I ran my hand over his thick messy hair. He was as tall as me and would catch up and pass his older brother in no time. "Come inside." I opened the clinic door. "I'll call Michael to come down and get you."

"Mom," he snickered. "I can walk home."

"I know. Come inside, we'll share." I opened the bag. "It smells so good."

"It's Patsy's."

We walked inside and no sooner did we hit the waiting room, Maryanne brushed by.

"Thank God you're finally here," she said. "Dr. Singh is in the back with Mrs. Snyder and an impacted ingrown toenail."

Eli groaned out.

I laughed at my son's reaction. "Okay, I'll just …"

Maryanne was out the door. No goodbye, just gone.

I placed the bag on the counter and pulled out the contents. "Burger and fries. Want half?"

"If you want," Eli said.

"Of course, I won't eat it all." I sniffed the burger. "Oh, wow, this is fresh. I'm gonna run to the back and get some napkins." I pointed. "Want a drink?"

"Orange soda if you got it."

"We do." I wanted to be quick, just in case someone came in. The small employee break room was in the back, not that we ever ate in there. I hurried in, grabbed some napkins, opened the fridge and pulled out the sodas.

"Clare, that you?" Sam called out.

"Yeah. I'm here." I stepped from the break room.

Sam popped his head out of room two. "Hey. When Mrs. Snyder is done …"

"Mom?" Eli called with question.

We both looked.

"Eli brought me lunch."

Sam nodded. "That's fine, but listen when I'm done, I really need to speak to you about something. Show you something. Okay?"

"Am I in trouble?"

"Mom."

I turned my head to the direction of Eli. "Be right there."

"You're not in trouble. It's important," Sam said. "Okay?"

"Yes. When she is done, I'll find you."

"Mom?"

What was up with Eli? He was usually quiet and submersed in a video game.

I returned to the waiting room, noticing through the corner of my eye that he was by the door. "What's going on?" I placed the sodas on the counter.

"The guy was driving really weird and now he's headed this way."

"I wonder if he's hurt?" I walked toward the door, pulling Eli back. Just as I arrived back the door flew open.

A man staggered through, he breathed heavily, his face red and flushed, his eyes pale.

"Help me," he said.

Before I could reach him he dropped to the floor. I noticed when he hit the ground his nose was bleeding.

"Eli, run and get Dr. Singh, tell him someone collapsed."

Eli took off and I lowered down to the floor. "It's okay. It's alright. The doctor will be right here."

"Can't breathe. Body hurts." Suddenly his arms pulled back close to his chest as in atrophy, his neck arched and he began to convulse.

"Sam!" I cried out.

"Clare!" I head Sam's voice, strong and firm. "Don't touch him." His voice drew closer until I saw he was in the waiting room. 'Don't touch him. He may have the fever."

My eyes widened as my heart sunk.

Too late.

My hands were already on the man.

EIGHT – SEALED

"Stay back!' Sam ordered. He secured a mask over his mouth, pulled on gloves as he walked to the door. "Eli, go in the reception office, shut the door and do not come out."

"Yes, sir," Eli said.

Sam immediately locked the door.

"What's going on?" I asked.

"Back away from him, Clare."

"But you don't know." I stood and backed up. "Sam?"

Sam crouched by the man. "He's still alive. Burning up." He tilted his head left to right. "Ears are bleeding. I do know. Tell Mrs. Snyder to stay in that room. We have a fifteen foot aerosol contamination area."

"How ... how do you know?" I asked breathlessly.

"It's what I wanted to talk to you about," he said. "Go to my office, there's an email on my desk. Call the number. Report this, then grab gloves and a mask and help me move him. For God's sake, make sure Eli is away."

"Yes. Right away." I spun on my heels, nervous as could be. Every part of me shook and I raced to Sam's office. When Mrs. Snyder asked, "What about my toe?"

I responded, "Stay in there, don't move or come out."

I ran into the small office. Right there on his desk was the printed email.

The heading: Health Alert.

Warning H7N2, also known as: European Respiratory Distress, Whitby Fever, has reached dangerous pandemic levels. We are attempting to minimize the impact in the United States.

It went on to list symptoms.

But where was the number?

Then I saw it, after the paragraph. 'Should you have a suspected case of H7N2, secure your facility to prevent further spread, and contact this number immediately.'

It was insane, while every branch of the government, social media outlet and news stations tried to make me out as a joke, it was no more than a feint for what was really happening.

The fever was real, it was spreading, and I was the ultimate diversion.

I dialed the number expecting a human, not an automated service.

Press one if you have a suspected case of H7N2....

Pressed.

Press one if you are a hospital or nursing home facility, two if you are a private practice, three if you are a clinic or ...

Pressed.

Please enter your zip code.

Entered.

At the tone, please state your address, when finished press pound.

Are you fucking kidding me? This was how it was handled? I left the address, pressed pound, only to hear, 'Thank you. Please keep patient isolated and an immediate quarantine on your facility until officials arrive."

End of call.

To me, the call was just some sort of statistic keeping formality. I believed we would end up calling emergency services and an ambulance would come and take the mystery man to the hospital.

We had four exam rooms so I went into the last one for gloves and a mask.

"Clare?" Mrs. Snyder called out. "What about my toe?"

I remained calm, in case I was contagious I paused outside of Mrs. Snyder's room. "We have a medical emergency. Please do not come out. It's important."

"What about my toe?"

I didn't have time. Rushing, I made my way to the waiting room. Sam was standing above the man, his gloved hand rested on top of his tossed black hair, and Sam looked shaken.

"He stopped convulsing," I said.

"Yes, well, he's dead."

I gasped in shock.

Eli's head popped up in the receptionist window. "He's dead?"

"Eli!" I swung and pointed back at him.

"You mean that man, right there is dead?" he asked. "I didn't realize people died that fast and quiet."

"Eli, please, stay back. You don't need to look." I told him.

"I never seen a dead man. I have to look."

"Eli! Oh my God. Stop." I turned back to Sam. "What now?"

"Let's carry him to a back room," Sam whispered, then lifted his head to my curious son. "Eli, do you know how to work a computer and printer?"

Eli snickered. "Um, yeah, I'm twelve, they teach that stuff in school."

"Good." Sam nodded. "Once me and your mother move him, I need you to make a sign for the door. Have it say we're closed for today and add the word 'sorry'. Can you do that?"

"Should I put it's because a man died in the waiting room?"

"No. Only ... that we're closed," Sam said.

"Okay. Cause it may keep people away and stop ...."

"No. Just the sign," Sam said, then looked at me. "Ready?" he asked "Take the legs and I'll take the shoulders."

I inched my way to his feet and that was when I really got another look at the poor man. Not only did he have fresh blood on his nose and ears, there was dried blood as well. His face was so pale and gray. I crouched down and grabbed hold of his calves.

"What's going to happen?" I asked Sam.

"I don't know. You made that call right?"

He counted to three, we lifted the man and began to carry him back.

"Yeah, I called, but it was automated."

"For real?"

I nodded. "We have to figure something out. Honestly, I don't think anything will come of that call."

I couldn't have been more wrong.

NINE – SWARM

His name was Fred Price, a forty-four year old man from Charleston, West Virginia. We got that from his driver's license.

He had business cards in his pocket with his name on them, Fred was a slot machine sales rep. Video Amusement device specialist. I suppose he was on his way to the resort or even staying in town. We didn't know.

Fred died in our little urgent care office. His last two words were, "help me," and we couldn't even do that.

How long did he suffer? According to the health alert, symptoms show up within two to three days of exposure. It begins with a slight headache, low grade fever and body aches. Each symptom increasing in intensity.

A highly contagious airborne virus.

It arrived in Mills Run via a traveling salesman.

Unfortunately for Mills Run, not only did the virus show up, but two reporters remained in town, living it up at the Mills Run hotel and making daily trips to the casino as if it were a vacation. Sticking around… just in case. I didn't understand the 'just in case', surprisingly they were there when the Center for Disease Control arrived in full force, toting a military escort.

I called that hotline at ten minutes after twelve and before one, the Sherriff arrived, slapped a yellow sign on the door and waved to us. Then he called to tell us not to leave.

That was before everything but the electricity was shut down.

Sam brought his charger and I was glad, because Eli's phone started to die, he at least had that for games. They cut the internet and phone lines to the clinic. My cell phone wouldn't make a call, no one's would.

I still don't know how they managed that. At least I got one text out to my father and Michael letting them know what was going on. I didn't say much, just that the Quick Med was under quarantine.

By four pm, the forces of health showed up in our parking lot. It was as if they were waiting somewhere all ready to go.

Plastic was placed all over the Quick Med building after they erected two connecting quarantine tents, they ran a tent hallway to our door and opened it. There was another door at the end of that hall. Admittedly, I didn't understand how that worked. How they kept contaminated air in one place and away from the other. Maybe there was some sort of decontamination beyond the connecting hall.

Shortly after all that was erected, they came and removed Fred's body.

Nothing was said to us. Men and women in space suit looking outfits told us to sit tight. Because Mrs. Snyder was nowhere near Fred Price, they asked me, Sam and Eli to keep clear of her and keep her in the exam room.

My father arrived at the building, I could hear him outside before I saw him. He was trying to figure out what was going on. Hell, I was trying to figure that one out, too.

They wouldn't even let him close enough to talk. I didn't understand why it was an issue. I did hear the one soldier tell him he would be able to in a little bit.

Time crawled. We heard nothing.

No one came in, nor brought us anything. We had to rely on chips, candy, crackers and soda from the employee room. All four of us shared that Pasty burger and fries, I reheated it in the microwave. I used gloves and placed Mrs. Snyder's share just outside exam room one. I felt bad for her. We at least had room to move. She was stuck in there. We couldn't even finish her ingrown toenail procedure. The poor thing. She didn't complain about her small room, she did complain about her toe.

It wasn't bad for all of us.

Sam slept. He said he was taking advantage of the fact that it was the longest break he had in awhile.

Without internet access, Eli was limited on his games. All the way into night fall he and I sat together in the waiting room, trying to peek through that recently erected hall way to see what the people in space suits were doing. To me they were just moving about like everyone else outside.

Tall spotlights were erected, illuminating the area as if it were daylight, and reporters and news trucks crowded the perimeter of the parking lot behind the barricade wooden horses.

It was a circus.

Finally, Eli fell asleep. I took his phone and put it on the charger, covering him with a blanket. I even got one for Sam. I checked on Mrs. Snyder to see if she was alright, she said she was so I settled down for the night on the sofa with my son. I had concluded we weren't hearing anything until morning.

Somewhere after midnight, Eli's head pressed tightly to my thigh, my hand on his hair, I dozed off. It wasn't for long because I was woken by a tapping. A continuous tapping. It stirred me awake and at first I thought I was dreaming when I saw Jael standing outside the waiting room window. I sat up and he waved at me with a huge smile.

"What the hell?" I walked over to him.

He pointed.

"What?" I lifted my hands.

Again, he pointed toward the door, then he walked away.

"What the hell?" I, too, walked toward the door and I saw him just outside the plastic window of the connecting tent hallway. As if I were doing something wrong, I quietly stepped into that hall.

"Hey," he said. "Can you hear me?"

I nodded. I could hear him, he was slightly muffled though.

"They said I could talk to you here."

"Oh," I sighed. "Good, I thought maybe you broke in the perimeter."

"Nah." He shook his head.

"What time is it?"

"Two thirty, I just closed the bar. Man, business was awesome. Anyhow, I promised your dad I'd come down and wait to see if they let me talk to you. I usually don't go to sleep early anyhow."

"They let you?"

"Obviously. They're keeping reporters back. Just family members now. Your dad and the kids will be down in the morning."

"Why did they let you in?" I asked. "Obviously we don't look like family."

He laughed. "I told them I was your husband."

"Good thing you're good looking or I'd be mad."

He smiled, then turned serious. "How are you?"

"Scared. We don't know if that man had it or not, no one is saying anything. I don't know how long we'll be in here."

"Four days."

"How do you know?" I asked.

"That's what they're saying on the news."

"Great. How much of a joke do I look like now?"

I watched him shake his head and exhale. "It was bad at first, you know. Everyone was saying you did this to make up for your hoax. It was an elaborate set up. Things started to shift when the CDC actually showed up. Still ... it was fifty-fifty, because the CDC was denying it and saying it was just a precaution. No fever here."

"That's a lie."

"It is. People believe now?"

"How?" I asked. "I mean, the government is denying it."

"It broke Clare. Whether this was how you wanted it to happen or not, the truth is out," Jael said.

"Are you serious?"

"The CDC is admitting that this thing is everywhere and now warnings are in effect, it's all over the news. They had to admit it when the proof went viral."

"What are you talking about?"

I watched Jael reach behind his back. "I had to print it for you since, you know, you don't have a phone." He unrolled a piece of paper and held it flush to the clear plastic. "Can you see that?"

"Oh my God." I looked at the paper. It was a printed article. Two pictures. On the left was a picture of me and Sam standing by Fred's body. On the right, was a zoomed in shot of Fred's virus stricken face. "Where did that come from?"

"Michael. He got a hold of one of the reporters in town. Eli sent it to him."

Quickly, I looked back to my sleeping son. "Oh, shit he took that from the reception window."

"Yep, sent it to his brother showing him the guy that died."

For all that I wanted to do to get the truth out, it was the innocence of my son's morbid curiosity that was the final nail of proof needed. Even though I was so relieved that I was no longer the internet's biggest joke, the whole entire scenario was suddenly real.

"What now?" I asked. "Are they saying?"

Jael shook his head. "No they aren't. They aren't even saying it's under control. Maybe now that the truth is out they can beat this thing."

"Let's hope. I saw what happened to that man, Jael," I said. "It's scary to think what will happen to his world if they can't get it under control."

TEN – HOLDING

April 5

An hour after they took blood from all of us, they removed Mrs. Snyder and took her into another area of the quarantine. Sam, me and Eli were deemed high risk.

"It was H7N2," said the doctor who spoke to us. "We need you for another four days, then you'll be free to go. We just need to take blood every day to see."

He never gave his name to us, no one did. Almost as if they didn't want to get close to us or know us.

Did they think we would get sick?

Before he left I had to ask him about the man who sent the message to me, "Do you know a Doctor Daryl Lewis?"

This made him pause. "How do you know that name?"

"I'm curious because I communicated with him," I said.

"He used to work with us, yes. Brilliant man. Could be the answer to all of this."

"So, he's working on a cure?" I asked.

"Sadly, for all of us, no," he replied. "He's in hiding somewhere waiting to die."

And that was it. That was all I got.

One would think being placed in quarantine, that we'd have all the answers. No one talked to us or told us anything. My one simple exchange was it and wasn't much help or information. If this Dr. Lewis could be the answer, it was disheartening to hear he wasn't working on the virus. A part of me wanted to reach out to him. Beg him to work on the virus. Even if it didn't work, it was worth a shot.

Quarantine was boring. They brought us food. At first it was pouches until local places started sending us meals.

My father was upset that they had us contained. While I wasn't happy about living in the Quick Med, I assured him I was alright with it because it was the responsible thing to do.

He understood and just as I got him calmed down, he was mad again because I failed to tell him my mother was coming to town.

She arrived late Sunday afternoon, after taking a flight to Pittsburgh, a cab ride to Steubenville, then caught my father's ferry. He of course, wasn't working and was shocked to see her standing at the quarantine window. Fortunately, she had made reservations before the reported ascended on Mills Run.

"What the hell are you doing here, Melinda?" he asked.

"I am visiting my daughter," she said. "Also, my grandchildren."

"Well isn't that swell of you. How long are you staying?"

"I don't know."

"What do you mean you don't know?" My father asked. "Don't you have a made for TV movie to do or something."

"I am here to add moral support for our daughter because I know what she is going through."

My father laughed. "How in the hell do you know what she's going through?"

"In the movie I just did, my character was quarantined from her family."

"Oh my God." My father turned and walked away.

I had to tell my mother to ignore him. My father was just sore because suddenly he wasn't the center of my kids' universe. They were all happy to see her and Eli didn't want her to go until after he was out.

It was funny to see my mother's version of dressed down. She always, for as long as I could remember dressed like the starlet she was. Until she came to Mills Run, whenever she visited she believed she needed to wear blue jeans and flannel. As if everyone in Ohio was a redneck or something.

The most positive thing about my mother's arrival was her power as a celebrity. Minutes after she arrived and started bitching to the press about our conditions, they had the internet up and running again, along with our phones.

Eli was glad, it gave him something to do.

Sam spent most of his time on the phone doing interviews with news outlets.

Me, I was happy because finally we weren't in the dark. While the doctors weren't telling us much, the news was.

It wasn't good.

Whitby Fever or ERDs was out there, it landed on American soil and each day it brought higher and higher numbers of infected. They didn't say how many died. The lack of information there told me more than any numbers would have. It had to be out of control.

Certain flights were suspended indefinitely, travel restrictions were in place, even trains weren't running on full schedule.

"Things will return to normal," the President said. "Just be proactive and trust we will get this under control."

I wasn't sure that was possible.

It was like watching a movie, it wasn't real because we weren't truly a part of reality while in quarantine. We could only watch from the sidelines.

While we were cooped up in a Quick Med urgent care, the world was rapidly changing as it faced an extinction level virus.

Mills Run and surrounding towns seemed under the radar of this deadly invasion. Other than Fred Price, there weren't any cases. However, with the way the virus moved and how fast it was, I knew that it wouldn't be long before that fatal virus found us.

ELEVEN – FACTS

April 7

I was fearful and I had to keep reminding myself that with every news worthy event it takes over the media and stays there for a week. Every social media is filled with the subject, right and left wing news outlets covered the same story differently. It reaches a plateau and then dies down. It's easy to remember when you aren't the center of the story.

It wasn't an ideal situation. They brought us some cots. I found the couches more comfortable. At least they tried to make it better.

We never saw Mrs. Snyder again. She stayed in the other tent because she was nowhere near Fred Price. I did hear they finished her ingrown toenail.

We went in on a Saturday and were told we'd be out on Friday.

It was a long week,

Eli's school was really understanding. They sent him work on Monday, so it wasn't a vacation, by Tuesday he was logging in and being part of the classes via a video stream. He didn't get off easy, but I did. Sam helped him with his work.

Sam was bored. This was a man who was constantly busy and when he wasn't he was drinking. In the quarantine, he drank a lot. He wasn't an alcoholic, but what else was there to do.

I read as much as I could and watched a lot of news. Too much news.

That swell of intensity over the news started to get big on Sunday and by Tuesday, if you asked me, I would have told you that the world was going to end.

"The world isn't going to end," Sam said to me that night. Eli was sleeping and we were playing a board game. "Trust me. This planet has been around a long time."

"Oh my God, I am not saying it's going to blow up. I'm saying that this is it. This is the big one that wipes out most of the population."

Sam tossed the dice. "I can't tell you how many times I have heard that before."

"Yeah, well, when have you heard of a virus wiping out domestic pets, one where species has no boundaries?"

He looked up in a questioning manner.

I knew he hadn't a clue. He wasn't reading the news. The veterinary clinic in South Carolina didn't stop there. Nineteen animals that went into the clinic that day during and after Harry's visit all died. Their owners were also infected.

It hadn't stopped.

Closer to home in the town of Wheeling, a Golden Retriever was diagnosed with having H7N2. His owner didn't have a clue how he came in contact with it. According to Freedom Righter, that owner died of the fever. Although the official cause was stated as heart failure. In Wheeling alone, over one hundred pets were euthanized for suspected H7N2, or for having it.

Ordinances were in place where pets were not allowed on the streets. That owners were to surrender their pets if they suspected the animal of having H7N2.

I told all of this to Sam and then showed him a news article on how other major cities were placing the Pet Restraint quarantine in effect.

"It spreads faster by pets," I said. "If your dog has it, then chances are you will. They piss, shit everywhere, leaving the virus."

"Really, though, think about it. If this virus is transmitted by your family dog and that dog gets sick, like this quarantine, isn't surrendering the dog the responsible thing to? Not to mention the humane thing to do."

"We don't do it to people."

"That's because people understand the reality of spreading a virus. Not that it would matter to some."

"It seems severe to be required to surrender a dog if you only suspect they're sick."

"Again, it's the responsible thing to do. You won't get me playing animal advocate on this one. Human life, to me, is first and foremost. Besides, how many pets really have been diagnosed with it?" Sam asked.

"There's no official number. I looked. In Wheeling it was over one hundred dogs and cats. That's not only sad, it's scary."

"Okay," he said passively.

"You don't have a pet, do you?'

"I have a hamster. He's probably dead now. Take your turn." He pointed to the board.

"That hamster could have it." I rolled the dice.

"Clare, a pet extinction is sad, it doesn't mean the end of humanity."

"I beg to differ," I said. "I saw movie four of Planet of the Apes. Conquest of the Planet of the Apes. The end of the world started with a dog and cat virus."

"Stop." Sam shook his head. "You're basing your end of man theory on a movie. Just stop."

"What if it is the one, Sam?" I asked. "Is there any way to survive?"

"You mean if this is the black plague on steroids?" He shrugged. "Isolation is the only way to outlive it, then again, that's not really a guarantee. Everyone has been waiting for the one. This isn't it."

I wanted to believe Sam's words, after all, he was the medical professional. No matter what I said he was going to argue with me. I was alright with that because I wanted him to argue with me. I needed him to prove me wrong.

How many times in the past did the CDC declare a virus or flu hitting epidemic proportions, or even declare something was pandemic?

The words are both frightening. Knowledge is key. Sam had me research while I fought bouts of neuroticism, the true meaning of epidemic and pandemic. Both were determined by the amount of cases in a short period of time. Pandemic would be over more than one country.

To be an epidemic there needs to only by fifteen cases of a flu or virus in a two week period in a population of 100,000. When thinking about it with those parameters, it wasn't much.

Our entire area, Weirton, Wheeling, Steubenville, Mills Run, and Sistersville, that was close to a hundred thousand, and only fifteen needed to be sick. When looking at that, epidemic wasn't quite so scary.

Statistics took the punch out of it.

The Spanish flu and black plague, they were synonymous with the word pandemic. Yet, there was an extinction level plague thousands of years earlier. The Plague of Justinian. Half the world's population died.

Half.

Not all.

In my mind, worst case scenario, if Whitby Fever was 'The One', then it would do what other historical extinction level pandemics did. It would bring countries to their knees, struggling to emotionally rebuild amidst the chaos of loss and economic collapse. It wouldn't be a handful of survivors walking around a barren world like so many books or movies portrayed. That was improbable, history proved that.

Finally, I had a more positive outlook, one that was less hysterical. I felt better.

When looking at it intelligently and armed with scientific facts, it was easier to face. The Whitby fever, while deadly and scary was not the end of the world.

It would have to run its course. Even if it hit really bad, I was confident because of limited access and back roads, that our small town of Mills Run would make it through just fine.

TWELVE – NORMALCY

April 10

Sam gave me strength.

In a sense, he schooled me.

The days in quarantine were informative and enlightening. Before the fever, I paid little attention to what went on in the world. My obsession with the outbreak caused me to thrive on reading and believing every single conspiracy site as if it were gospel.

Then in a matter of days, I was reasonable again. Dismissing the outlandish claims about the flu and listening to the realistic ones.

Yes, my friend Nick died. It was heartbreaking. The UK suffered horribly with the Whitby fever, but from what I heard and read, it was finished over there. Any other reports were just sensationalized.

I truly one hundred percent believed that.

It was the only way to think or else I would drive myself insane.

Eventually, it would be over.

Two days before we were released, one of the doctors actually spoke to me. None of them had, we were mere subjects. He told me how the fever virus wasn't really that easy to catch from another person. The animal species form spread faster to humans.

Suddenly I was the voice of reason with the virus. Even more so than Sam. A complete one eighty. When he brought up that more dogs and cats were infected, I brought up that the government was being proactive.

I bought into it one hundred percent.

The government told us we were fine … why would I dismiss it.

Things seemed to settle in the days we were in quarantine. It went from being the responsible thing to do to something really silly and I wanted out. I missed my kids, wanted to work and was pissed Jael was making all my money.

Two days before we were released, they started pulling out. Sam and I began the task of cleaning the Quick Med, believing everything would be back to normal. It wasn't. While most of the medical staff had left along with the military, they left their tents and barricades, almost as if they were expecting to return.

The morning of our release, they took a blood test and after an hour, opened the doors.

Apparently, they let Mrs. Snyder go, because we never saw her. The impact the virus had with the news and social media started to die down. Interest waned even though news sites posted daily statistics on infected people and pets from major cities.

The numbers seemed small and it wasn't frightening.

Los Angeles one thousand human cases.

New York … two thousand. Really, in comparison to the population that was nothing.

I wasn't worried and it seemed no one else was anymore.

Except Trevor. He would text me, "They say it's carried in all animals and rodents."

"Let it go," I replied. "This isn't the one."

"If that's the case they'll never be able to track the route of infection."

"Let it go."

I didn't want to hear it or read it. I had resolved myself that this was just another seasonal mishap, a little bigger than others, but nothing to neurotic over.

We walked out to no fanfare. A few reporters asked how we felt, not even my father was there. I suppose he was working. Life went on.

We went from being in the spotlight to an afterthought. That was fine with me.

Sam's car wouldn't start so one of the reporters gave him a jump. He had to head back to Steubenville, take a real shower and check on his dead hamster.

Eli and I headed home on foot. It wasn't that far and the weather was nice.

It felt weird to be out, to walk past the quarantine area around the Quick Med.

"You think they'll take this down?" Eli asked.

I looked at the barricade horses, the tents and litter in the parking lot. "I hope. This is pretty scary."

"Where is everyone?"

"Working I guess" I answered quickly.

The town of Mills Run was oddly quiet for noon. Only a few people were on the streets and maybe two cars passed us. Perhaps we got used to all the buzz with the reporters.

It was suddenly gone.

I just wanted to get home, get clean and lay on my own bed. I wanted to hold Ivy and Michael. I had spoken to them through a plastic window, but I missed them.

We walked by Hap's Barber shop, he was doing a haircut and waved as we walked by. Aside from the low key feel of the town, I believed nothing had changed, until I noticed the signs.

There was something different in Mills Run after all.

The yellow signs posted on telephone poles and store windows.

They were a warning that I didn't expect to see in my home town. The residents of Mills Run were told that in according to a new federal law, domestics pets were not allowed off of private property. Any animal found in public would be seized, impounded and disposed of.

For the health and welfare of all.

It was a reality check that the threat of the virus was still there. It was heartbreaking to think what was being done to the animals, to beloved pets that had been part of families. In my mind, even though it was sad, drastic measures or not, it was proactive, and what needed to be done to stave off the virus.

I truly believed it was only a matter of time before it was done and we'd go back to living life normally.

THIRTEEN – CHANGES

For all my mother's cooking shortcomings, she did make amazing fried chicken. My father's house smelled glorious when I arrived. I wondered if my father knew she was there?

I embraced my mother with gratitude and laughed about her choice in flannel.

"I would have come down to get you," she said. "But they didn't give me a time, so I figured, I would make a big meal we can all share tonight. Good thing I didn't wait. The market is only open for a few hours a day."

"Really?" I asked. "Why?"

"The virus, fever. People are being cautious."

"Not so cautious that the schools are still open."

"A lot of people are sick. It won't be long if it continues like this. "

"I'm trying not to think like that," I said. "I'm trying to put myself in the mindset that this will be over and we'll emerge unscathed. I have to or I'll drive myself nuts. So, …" I exhaled. "I look at it scientifically and historically. I've been locked in a bubble reading what I can. What has it been like? How are people handling things?"

My mother shrugged. "They're afraid, but I think everyone is thinking like you. Except those sites which are showing pictures of body bags." She shuddered. "I hope those pictures are fake. I really do."

I did, too. I nodded and gave her my assurance that I believed they were. Not that I knew any better. As I told her, I was locked in a bubble. I would have a better idea once I was out and about.

Eli wanted to spend time with my mother and they worked on peeling potatoes for the salad, while I showered then headed up to Steubenville to get Ivy and Michael from school.

The drive would be informative. Mills Run was such a small town it was hard to gauge what was going on elsewhere by what happened in our town.

Not that Steubenville was a booming metropolis but it was bigger than Mills Run. The roads were pretty clear with very little traffic. It had that 'day after Labor Day' feel to it, less people. Starbucks was open, of course. Everything was open in Steubenville. Like Mills Run, those yellow pet control signs were everywhere, however one thing was different. There were a lot of people wearing surgical masks. The baristas at Starbucks wore them along with gloves.

A few people on the street sported the masks, the school crossing guard in front of the high school, as did several of the students. It was obvious while I was in quarantine learning my facts, everywhere else was gripped by the fear of the fever.

<><><><>

My father was in one of those moods when he returned home. I heard him complaining about the neighbor's dog before he even opened the back door.

"There are laws now!" my father shouted, I could only guess it was at the neighbor. "Keep that mutt in your yard, or I'll shoot him myself." He walked in and slammed the door.

We all were seated at the kitchen table, just waiting on him and we all just stared at him.

"Dog was in the yard again." He cleared his throat.

"Pappy, would you really shoot the dog?" Ivy asked.

"Yes, yes, I would."

"Dad!" I blasted.

"No, Clare, I'm serious. Animals are spreading this thing. There's a reason for the yellow signs."

"Even if he's not sick?" I asked.

"Some don't show symptoms." My father paused and finally noticed that we were all seated around a set table. His eyes shifted to my mother.

"Did you want a drink, John?" She asked him. "Maybe calm down some."

"Why are you playing house in my home?" He sat down.

"Dad, don't be mean to mom," I said.

"Sorry, just a bad day. Yes, Melinda, I would love one and I smell chicken."

"Sort of a welcome home for Clare." She handed him a beer, then sat as well. "Why was your day so bad?"

"No one wants to work except Jael. He's not good enough to run the casino trips." He shook his head. "We're down twenty five percent this week in passengers. Second engine was acting up and I just replaced the damn thing, Then I come home to find that damn dog in my yard."

"You know," Michael said. "I heard that it's not the animals spreading it, but the people giving it to the animals."

I nodded. "I believe that. That's how Harry Davis got it and died. His dog got it from the boat people and gave it to him."

My father set down his beer. "What are you talking about? Who is Harry Davis?"

"He's the man that found the boat of refugees last month in Florida," I said. "He started it all."

"Then I blame Harry Davis for affecting my business."

"It'll take awhile for things to quiet down," my mother said, passing the plate of chicken. "Probably a good month before things go back to normal. I mean, this things spreads fast, people show symptoms quickly, something like this will take two weeks of no cases before they declare an area flu free."

"When did you become an expert?" my father asked.

"That movie I just did," she replied. "It was a very similar virus and the writer did lots of research. Very smart man."

"Speaking of movies," my father said. "Don't you have one to film or a TV show to do?"

"Dad," I scolded.

"I'm just asking. She's been here nearly a week."

"I'll be here longer," My mother said. "With that travel ban, there's no flights out of infected areas. I have to fly out of Pittsburgh, it's an infected area."

"See, I don't get that." My father pointed his fork. "What's to stop someone from driving out of an infected area."

"If it gets any worse, the news said they'll be quarantines," Michael said. "They didn't sell prom tickets this week and they said we may not go back after Easter break."

"Guys," I said with a chuckle. "They are over reacting."

My father nearly choked. "Clare, you flip more on this virus than anyone I met. One day it's the end, the next day everyone's exaggerating. Make up your mind."

"I just did a lot research when I was quarantined and watched the news."

"Well, maybe you're only reading and learning what you want to read and learn. We're lucky here in Mills Run, but outside of here, tens of thousands have it. People are dying from it. They aren't getting better."

I shifted my eyes to Ivy. "Maybe we shouldn't talk about this right now?"

"We should. It's scary," Eli said. "That man that died had it. He looked bad."

"Yeah," Ivy said. "It made me scared."

I looked at my daughter. "You saw the picture?"

Ivy pointed to Michael. "He showed me."

"She asked," Michael defended. "Besides, Eli took the picture."

"It was the first dead guy I saw," Eli said. "I had to show you."

"Too bad you didn't see Mrs. Snyder," Michael said. "That would have been two."

"Michael, Sweetie," I reached over and tapped his hand. "Mrs. Snyder isn't dead."

"Yeah, she is mom, we watched them carry her body out."

I looked to my father. "Is she dead? How did she get the fever?'

"Wasn't the fever," my father replied. "Said she had an infection which caused a heart attack."

Somehow a part of me just didn't believe it. Mrs. Snyder was in quarantine with us and she died from a heart attack. I excused myself from the table for a moment with my phone in my hand, I walked into the other room to call Sam.

"I thought you'd be tired of me," Sam said as he answered the phone.

"She died, Sam."

"My hamster? No it's still alive."

"No, Mrs. Snyder. She died. My family just told me they watched them take her body out. Did you know?"

"No…. I'm in shock, Clare, are you sure?" he asked.

"Positive. They're saying it was a heart attack. Could it have been the fever and they are covering it up?"

I expected a quick reply, maybe Sam would be rational and tell me that there was no way it was the fever, instead I got a different answer.

"It's possible. It would explain why we were in quarantine that long when the incubation is at most two days."

"Why would they cover it up and lie?"

"To stop panic," Sam said.

"Sam," I said nearly breathless. "We talked a lot about this. You said this isn't the big one."

"And I stand by that. I'm not saying it isn't going to be bad."

"Sam?"

"There's a few cases in Steubenville. It's not public yet."

"How many?"

"A few. Nine suspected cases," he said. "My father said there hasn't been any in the last twenty-four hours, which is a good thing."

"Sam ... that guy in the clinic, was he a fluke ... or are people dying from this?"

Pause.

"Yeah, Clare, this fever is a killer."

"Oh my God."

"Listen to me. It's nine cases. We can't panic, you can't get back in that 'end of the world' mode again. You can't. You'll drive yourself nuts. Don't let this dictate your life, go on as normal. There's no reason to be scared. We'll know for certain in a few days."

"What will we know?"

"If it's going to fade away or ... get worse. I believe," he said. "The worst is over."

I listened to his reasoning, his expertise opinion. I was going to take his advice and not panic again, stay calm and be optimistic about it all. What else I could I do? The alternative outcome was just to maddening to comprehend.

FOURTEEN – SAWING

April 13

Why didn't I listen to my father? Over Sunday dinner he tried his hardest to convince me to keep the kids home from school. I couldn't justify it. From what I had read and hear, new cases of the fever hadn't spiked and the president was encouraging everyone to go about as normal as possible. If we didn't, things would economically collapse. Not that sending my children to school had an economic impact, but it was all in the course of going about our lives as normally as possible.

Eli hadn't been to school in over a week. He had to go back. He wanted to. Easter break was a few days away and really, what could happen in those few days?

I felt like a fool.

Sitting in the school parking lot, reading that email stating school would be closed indefinitely, looking around. The emptiness, the frightened parents. A few minutes earlier I thought it was merely odd that only a very few children emerged from school. Now I found it frightening. I stared at the playground, watching the swings move slightly with the breeze. Would it ever be normal? The sight of that swing set just broke my heart.

Please, I prayed in my mind, *let those children be all right.*

My child could very easily have been one of them.

The fever killed. I knew that from Sam.

My hands clutched the steering wheel as my veil of delusion was lifted and I faced a gray world. I had spent weeks being a town crier, the Chicken Little of the virus raged world. Instead of screaming, "The sky is falling, the sky is falling." I cried out, "We're all gonna get sick and die."

In that screaming and ranting, I failed to see that I, that my family could be a part of the statistics. Perhaps it was that reality which made me take a complete one eighty. I submerged myself in total disbelief as some sort of protection against the deadly possibility.

However, no denying the intensity of the fever was going to lessen the reality of it.

More than ever, in the after moments in the parking lot, I saw the emptiness of the closed shops I passed on the way to get Ivy, and the missing cars. I recalled my conversation with Marcia at Starbucks. She was saying something about the fever, about closing, I failed to really listen.

The news was even different. I wasn't imagining that. It went from "act normal", to "if it at possible, avoid public places."

What was happening?

Was it really that fast, or had I just blinded myself?

"Mommy?" Ivy called my name. "Can we go home?"

I snapped out of it. We were the last car in the parking lot.

"Mommy, is everything okay?"

I peered up to the rearview mirror, looking at my innocent daughter. She asked if everything was okay. I forced a smile and life. "Yes. Everything is fine."

<><><><>

I could hear the distance sirens from across the river as they cut through the dead silence of the night. An odd quiet to Mills Run, no car sounds, no people talking on the street nor the hourly fog horn blast of my father's ferry.

The sirens were always heard before, but I never really paid attention to them. Suddenly they took on new meaning. Was someone hurt? Did they have the fever?

I didn't want to leave the house, but I needed to see if I could make some money and take my mind off of things. Both were fails.

People heeded the new warning to stay away from public places and the Pepper Mill was empty except me, Jael and Sam.

As for not thinking about the virus, that was hard to do. The news told the same story over and over with different experts saying the same thing. I would have turned it off, yet I waited for the rare person on the news to say it wasn't all bad.

It was.

The advisories weren't mandatory, yet, more than likely they would be. The news told what to do if you suspect you have the fever, and also, the stories of the needless euthanizing of thousands upon thousands of household pets willingly surrendered just as a precaution.

Jael didn't say much, he watched the news. He was in a constant battle with Sam. The volume of the television versus Sam's choice in music. Sam was odd, I had never seen him act like he was. Careless, drinking even more heavily, and hugging the jukebox almost pathetically every time a song would start.

It took about the fifth or sixth song for me to realize what he was doing. I didn't figure it out on my own, Jael said something. The moment the song, *'End of the world as we know it'* began, Jael snapped. "Sam, come on really. Stop with the apocalypse songs."

That's when it hit me, it was all he played.

Eve of Destruction, Don't fear the Reaper, Sound of Silence.

Sam waved out his hand to Jael. "I never knew the words to this song. They just fly by so fast." He walked to the bar, pausing and looking at the television. "They do have a point about that. Stay away from crowds."

"Will that really work?" Jae asked. "I mean, isn't it airborne?"

Sam nodded. "Yeah, it's not like it flows through your kitchen window. Unless someone coughs out there with it. The air dissipates it. Theoretically, self-quarantine will stop it. Like most viruses, this doesn't live on tissue more than fifteen minutes. So, the dead don't carry it. Surfaces up to twenty-four hours with each hour the virus weakens it. In the air, a couple hours top. Again, time weakens it so...." He sat on a stool. "If everyone locked themselves in a room, away, and waited until everything that has it dies. Dogs, people, rodents, insects, two weeks. Then a few more days, the virus would be done. People won't do that. So it spreads." He pushed his glass to me. "Another."

"Aren't you driving?" I asked.

"Nope. I am here in Mills Run for the duration. Booked the Lincoln Suite. I won't be working in Steubenville, Pittsburgh, or Weirton when they make it mandatory for medical personnel to stay at the hospital. The more people that get it, the more chance there is I will be waiting in a hospital watching the world die."

"So, why here?" I asked, pouring a drink.

"Less chance of it hitting, and if it does ... where are the people of Mills Run going to go? The Quick Med is it. Send them to Steubenville? What happens if they get stuck there. No. I stay." He sipped his drink. "Do you know what it's like to be a know it all? To think you have this thing figured out and you're wrong. Oh!" he chuckled. "Yeah, Clare you do. I did that to you. I'm sorry."

"What are you talking about?" I asked. "You handed me facts. We looked at history. We believed what we wanted to believe." I poured myself a drink, then one for Jael. "What about you, Jael? You seem so indifferent."

"What can you do?" he shrugged. "I mean, I am not going to drive myself nuts. It is what it is. You can't change it, no matter how hard you try. The only thing about this virus that we can control is how we deal and act. Other than that, it's out of our hands."

"It's bad," Sam said. "Steubenville has less than twenty-thousand people and twenty percent have it. Pittsburgh has hit twenty-thousand cases. Where are they putting all the bodies, all the sick? The hospitals aren't equipped to handle them. They're supposed to move med camps up there so people can get medicine and die at home."

"Medicine to die at home?" I asked. "I know this fever kills, but not everyone. Some will get better, right?"

"No one gets better. Yeah, there's no coming back from this thing. The only thing is medicine to make it tolerable. The young, the old, they're lucky. They go fast from the fever. The strong ... they get the respiratory thing and have it bad."

"Sam, you're scaring me," I said.

"I'm sorry. I don't mean to. This comes from my father. The news..." he pointed to the television. "Won't tell you that. They say take ibuprofen. Me, if I get it, I wanna run a direct IV with Jack Daniels into my veins and go out that way."

"We talked about plagues and the history of them," I said. "So, this isn't another one of those events?"

"My worry is, if this continues at the current rate, increasing day by day, then just like the Justinian Plague, the world will get a population reset with this one. The sad part is, everyone..." he then emphasized. "*Everyone*, you, me....maybe not Jael because he doesn't have anyone. Everyone will eventually lose someone they love to this virus. We all just need to mentally prepare for that."

How? How does one mentally prepare to lose someone they love to a senseless virus? A burp of mother nature that went out of control. It was a thought I didn't even want to entertain. My children were my life. If I couldn't handle my husband's death, there was no way I was strong enough to live through something happening to one of my children.

There was no mentally preparing for that. None at all.

"We're lucky here, though," Jael said. "We're cut off."

Sam nodded. "That may be the saving grace of Mills Run and why there aren't any cases here."

"That we know of," Jael said. "I mean, how many of our people go to Steubenville, Weirton. Just the other day Gordon took ..."

He froze.

"What?" I asked. "What's going on?"

"Do you hear that?" he asked.

"No, I ..." Then I did. It sounds like a sawing noise. As if someone was sawing one way, hard and fast. I muted both the television and jukebox. The noise continued. "What is that?"

Jael stood. "Where is it coming from?"

Sam shook his head. "Is Gordon making something?"

"No, he should be sleeping. He's never up ..."

The three of us jumped when we heard what sounded like tumbling. Instantly, I was hit with that gut sinking feeling, someone or something fell down the inside stairs. It was followed by an immediate bang against the door. My focus zoomed in, like a camera, to the door across the bar in the corner, the one that led up to Gordon's home.

Jael was the first to fly over to the door. I know I thought the worst, Gordon had fallen down the stairs and at seventy-five years old that wouldn't be good.

When he opened it, the lifeless body of Gordon's German Sheppard, Maxi rolled out onto the floor.

I gasped and jumped.

"Don't touch her!" Sam yelled. "Don't. Back up. Ten feet."

"But Gordon ..." Jael said.

"One second. Back ... up." Sam instructed.

I quickly looked at Sam and he ran to the bar for his backpack.

I was already a good ten feet away, but it didn't stop me from seeing Maxi. They gray and white dog was on her back, eyes wide open, mouth as well. Her tongue extended out and was covered with blood. There was blood in her ears and her nose was crusted over.

"Put these on." Sam handed me a mask and gloves, then did the same to Jael. "Make sure it covers your nose and mouth, then bend the wire over your nose."

The mask was different than the ones at the Quick Med. It was circular and had a hard round piece center of it.

Sam bent down toward the dog. He looked ahead at the staircase. "Where did you say Gordon went?"

"He went to Pittsburgh. There's a vet there giving out boosters to help the pets, like a flu shot." Almost dazed, Jael walked to the door. "Oh my God, I haven't seen him since yesterday."

Sam reached out, stopping him. "Stay here. Let me go."

His warning wasn't heeded and Jael raced up the stairs.

"Clare, please stay." Sam looked back at me and then followed Jael.

Arms folded, I backed up. There I was in the middle of the bar, it seemed like Maxi was staring at me. Reaching over, I grabbed one of the green vinyl table clothes from a table, sending the salt shaker to the floor.

Cautiously, I stepped to Maxi and placed the table cloth over her. As the cloth draped over her lifeless body, I saw Sam slowly coming down the stairs.

He paused at the bottom, looked at me and slowly shook his head.

I blinked long and hard and brought my hand over my mask.

"Clare, call um ... the state police."

"The state police?"

"Yes, tell them a doctor is here and we need a coroner pick up. Please do so now."

I nodded.

Sam turned.

"Sam?"

He stopped.

"Was it …?"

"Yeah, it was the fever."

The second he confirmed my worst fears he went back up the stairs. I lost all breath. In fact, I hyperventilated and my hands shook.

Poor Jael. It was going to be devastating to him. Contrary to what everyone believed, he did have family, he had Gordon.

Now Gordon was gone.

I lifted the phone to call the police and realized from that moment on, everything was going to be different. Life just changed in an instant for everyone in Mills Run and most of the townspeople weren't even aware.

They would be soon enough.

FIFTEEN – SWIPE

When the world flipped a page, and like me suddenly realized what the fever virus was doing to our world, everything changed. The protocol on doing things was totally different, yet no one informed the public.

Gordon passed away and clearly it was from the fever. A week earlier the health alert gave a number to call, now that number wasn't valid.

There was no sweeping in of the CDC, no sheriff putting a sign on the door. There was nothing.

State Police wouldn't handle the call, nor would the country coroner. They were under instructions to not handle any fever infections. They did tell us to call the animal control number on the yellow signs in regards to Maxi. We were not to bury her ourselves. They also suggested calling an ambulance.

While Sam called animal control, I called for an ambulance even though we knew he had passed, they said it would be at least five hours.

The dispatcher suggested since we had a doctor on hand for them to pronounce the death. We could call a funeral home directly, then she said it could be difficult to find someone.

The state had placed a temporary stay on burials because not only was there not room to bury all the bodies with the sudden influx of dead, the funeral homes could not handle the incoming.

This wasn't happening.

"It's not like there's millions," she told me. "If ten times more people die a day in a city, that alone will cause the back up."

I thought of Ebola outbreaks and how the deceased were handled then. In largely affected areas, the typical funeral ritual was set aside.

They suggested we take Gordon to either Steubenville or Weirton, where health department officials had taken over body disposal.

It sounded so cold.

Since there were no funeral homes in Mills Run, I started calling the twenty-four hour hotlines of the ones in the area. The first three I spoke to told me the same thing. They weren't doing any embalming, viewings or funerals, they were performing cremations. The earliest they could get Gordon was the next afternoon.

Finally, Feeny's in Steubenville committed to picking up Gordon in an hour or so. They would perform the cremation after a seventy-two hour wait. We could go at the end of the week to pick up the remains.

Funny thing, there was no mention of cost, no financial arrangements. The man I spoke to stated their main concern was getting the bodies so as to halt any spread of other diseases.

My God, how many were there and why wasn't there any mention of it on the news?

Shortly before midnight, we learned that Gordon had died.

Animal control came for Maxi before I even finished making phone calls about Gordon. It was nearly three in the morning when Feeny's arrived. They asked for his driver's license or an ID card, and we could have it back when we retrieved his ashes.

It was for identification purposes.

While we waited for them, we talked. We tried to trace Gordon's path. Who he talked to, interacted with primarily the day before he died when he was contagious.

The receipts in his wallet told us he went from Pittsburgh straight home. He didn't do much outside of being at the bar. Even then he rarely interacted with customers, it was a good thing.

Chances were, hopefully, Gordon didn't pass the infection to anyone.

Sam was the first to leave and it wasn't long before I did. He said he wanted to get the Quick Med ready, just in case.

Jael and I locked the bar and hung a sign, 'Closed Indefinitely'.

I felt bad for Jael. I asked if he needed me to hang out with him. He didn't.

"I just need to absorb this. Process this. I'll be fine," he said. Then he offered to walk me the rest of the way home.

I didn't need him to. It was out of his way and only a few blocks. I needed the time as well to process.

I gave him a hug and told him I was there, to call me any time. He was my friend and despite what he put out there, he was hurting.

I walked at a steady slow pace, the evening wasn't too cold temperature wise, but it had an eerie feel to it. A chill that screamed calm before the storm.

On the way home I sent Trevor a text, telling him about Gordon. He had been irritated by me since my mindset flip flopped in quarantine. He really hadn't texted much at all except an occasional link about the virus in some sort of bid to anti-brain wash me and undo all that had been done to my thinking in quarantine. I didn't read them or look. I didn't need to. I told him I was being more realistic now, he didn't respond. Perhaps the Gordon text would prompt a reply.

My house was unusually bright when I got home, worrying me some, until I walked in and saw Eli playing video games in the living room.

"What are you doing up?" I asked.

"Pap said I could. I wanted to finish this game. Grandma stayed. She's in bed with Ivy."

"Swell, where am I supposed to sleep?"

He pointed to the couch. My pillow was there with a blanket.

"Not too much longer, okay? Either that or you'll have to play with headphones."

"Got it."

I leaned down and kissed him, then headed into the kitchen. I was hungry. If Eli hadn't told me my mother was there, I would have known. On the counter was a plate covered with plastic. It had a peanut butter and jelly sandwich, a handful of chips, a banana and note from my mother.

'Thought you'd be hungry after your night. I promise a good breakfast. Love, Mom.'

I grabbed my plate, a beer from the fridge and my tablet from the counter As I prepared to sit at the table, I noticed the back door was ajar, and the small bug light was on. I set down my plate, beer in hand and walked to the door.

Michael was just sitting on the back porch on the bench glider, staring out.

"Hey." I pushed open the screen door. "You're still up, too?"

"Waiting on you and I wanted to talk to Sophia. Video talk. Connection is bad in the house."

"I know." I sat next to him. "Thank you for waiting up. How's your girlfriend?"

"Good." He shrugged. "Her parents aren't letting her leave the house."

"That's not a bad thing, Mike. Dr. Sam said self-quarantine is the best, if we stay away long enough, we can beat this."

"This is all happening so fast."

"I know."

"I mean, one day everything is fine," Michael said. "The next everything is falling apart. People are getting sick and they're dying fast. It's scary."

"Scary being the definitive word."

"What are we going to do?"

I shook my head. "I don't know. Hating to sound cliché, but we hope for the best and prepare for the worst."

"Is that possible?" he asked. "To even prepare for the worst?"

"I don't think so." I took a drink from my beer bottle.

"Mom, I know I'm not that old, but I don't ever remember things shutting down like this. Has it ever happened before that you know of? I mean, where people thought the world was going to end?"

"It's happened with other countries, outbreaks. It's been scary before. Never on this level." I took another drink. "One time I did think the world was going to end. Me and your dad were just married and living in Buffalo. A major storm was coming and things shut down days before. We woke up literally buried in four feet of snow. No electricity, no phones. I swore the new ice age had arrived. Then life went on. As I suppose it will now. Just a lot differently."

Michael nodded as he understood what I was saying. "I'm sorry about Gordon."

"Thanks, I ... wait. How did you know?"

"Pap heard it on the scanner. Well, state police talking about not getting him. They were going back and forth on what to tell you. It's really sad."

"Yeah, it is."

"If more people get sick and die, then what?"

"I don't know."

"Well, I wanted to know. So, I was like, doing research..." he lifted his phone. "Looking up how they handled pandemics and dead before."

"Mass graves?" I asked.

"Yep." He nodded again and swiped open his phone. "There's been a lot of times in history. Some not that long ago. Ebola. The Indonesia tsunami. Then I found this. Take a look."

My initial thought was that my teenage son was being morbid, especially when I saw the first picture he showed me. A huge pit the size of a swimming pool. Bodies were covered, lined up and layered. They were lowering more down.

I swiped across to the next picture, it was more of the same. So was the next one. I wanted to scold him, tell him not to look, it would frighten him less. Michael wasn't a baby. He was intelligent and more mature than any teenager I knew. More than likely, he processed things better than me.

"There's four hundred million people in America," Michael said. "You look at those pictures and you think, wow, that's a lot of bodies."

"Well, it is a lot of bodies."

"That's what happens when eleven thousand people die really fast."

"Mike ..." I handed him the phone. "Please, I know you want to be informed, but looking at old pictures isn't going to help. Where was this taken? Is this from the tsunami?"

"No, mom, it's from the fever. It was taken today in Houston."

Quickly, I took the phone again and looked. The pictures weren't from some conspiracy site, they were from reputable news sources.

Staring at them brought even more of a cold reality. Michael had asked me if there was any way to really prepare for the worst. At that moment, I rethought my answer to him. While I didn't think there was a way, I knew I had better find one, we all had to find a way or else we were going to be in for a hard awakening, when, not if the fever virus hit its peak.

SIXTEEN – LAST AISLE

April 14

The sun was nearly up and Eli wrapped up his game by the time I was tired enough to fall asleep on the sofa. It wasn't long though before my father woke me.

He spoke to me in a whispering voice, clearly not wanting anyone to hear. "Clare, hey. Get up and get dressed. We have things to do." He nudged me. "Coffee's done."

"What time is it?"

"Seven."

"Jesus, dad, I just went to sleep."

"Well, you should have gone to sleep earlier. Come on, don't dally. We have to do this early."

I was barely off that couch, faced washed, when a travel mug of coffee was placed in my hand and we were out the door, hopping in his pickup.

He handed me a face mask and set the black case between us then opened it. I looked down to it in surprise. "I understand the mask. Why did you bring the pistols?"

"Because we're going shopping. Everyone is out there doing the same thing." He engaged a clip in the 9 mm and handed it to me. "Safety is on. Carry it behind your waist, when we go in. I'm hearing horror stores and don't pull it unless you intend to use it."

"Why are we going?" I asked. "I mean, we have food. I did my panic shopping before everyone was panicking."

"We need more."

"More?"

He started the truck and pulled. "We need enough. Soon there roads will be cut off. Towns will shut down. It's happening now in parts of this country. Before long it will happen here and I want us safe. Gordon won't be the only one."

"I think we are safe," I said. "I mean, we can cut ourselves off."

"The virus is here already. One person, two or a hundred, it's here."

I tossed out my hand. "So, nowhere is safe?"

"Yeah, there is."

"Where?"

"My boat," he said. "I want to take it south, where the river widens and just dock or shut down, wait it out."

"How long?"

"Two, three weeks."

"That's actually a really good idea. When did you want to do this? Tomorrow?"

My father shook his head. "No, you were by the dog last night, we're going out in public. No need to get on that boat if one of us is sick. We give it a few days, self-quarantine at the house and then head out. I started getting the ferry ready last night. We're topped off with fuel and water. We have everything we need."

The plan felt good. It could work, we could beat the virus if we avoided everyone and any exposure. What better way to do so than to take the ferry far from people. I wondered how many people had the same idea. Isolate themselves. Stay clear. Stay alive.

We listened to the radio for a short time as we headed toward the market in Weirton. The news talked about the virus, the intensity of it. Authorities urged people to avoid public places. We weren't listening, I guessed others weren't either. The roads were jammed packed and every business we passed had a line out the door.

If there would be a defining moment on when the virus spread, this would be it. Everyone was preparing for the worst and in doing so, opened themselves up to be exposed.

It wouldn't be long before people stopped venturing out, stores closed down, and the infrastructure just fell.

When that happened, I assumed violence and true panic would began, making the world an even more dangerous place.

My father stated that the super center would be the last place we'd go, if the smaller markets didn't work out. He felt they would be more crowded and more chances of trouble.

The medium size grocery store in Weirton opened at eight.

We arrived only a few minutes after and the lot was packed, and people were racing to the store as if some sort of bomb was going to fall at any second. So many people wore masks, my father and I were among them.

We found a buggy at the back of the lot, it was on its side and probably had rolled that way. We parked in the back, and moved quickly across the lot toward the store. More cars kept driving in, people had the same idea as my father.

The automatic doors didn't seem wide enough or open fast enough for the people that crammed in. The first display was for crackers and two boxes remained, the second I grabbed for one, it was gone.

We had to be faster.

We could barely move, pushed and shoved, people yelled quite a bit at each other. No one was bargain shopping, they were just grabbing items. They should have paid attention to the prices, everything was marked up incredibly high. So much so that people were shocked at the checkout. The store had just opened; how were there so many checking out?

As we moved into the main portion of the store, I could see and hear what was going on.

They shouted, *"This is insane. I'm not paying that.'*
"What are you doing, you can't take that?"

"One per customer."

There were six security guards, all doing their job and enforcing rules that weren't posted anywhere, at least anywhere I could see.

From observing just a few seconds of the happenings at the checkout, I knew there were limited items per customer, and if someone couldn't pay, they didn't get their food.

I watched a woman dragged out, kicking and screaming as her cart was taken away by security. I wondered why they held their posts so diligently. Were they promised a food order at the end of the day?

"Clare, let's go." My father tugged me, pulling my attention away from check out.

"I just want to make sure that doesn't happen to us."

"It won't."

A few feet into the store, I saw the first posted sign. It was two per customer on cereal. Those handwritten signs were everywhere, along with signs that read, "you steal we shoot."

"Can they get away with that?" I asked my father. "Marshal Law isn't in effect, how can they post that sign?"

"I don't know. I wouldn't want to test it or try it."

However, there weren't limits on produce, no one fought for that. We did. We took apples, oranges, onions, anything we could dehydrate over the next few days while we self-quarantined. We would do the same with meat.

We were doing pretty well until I saw it. The cardboard display with the happy cartoon rabbit holding a basket.

My mind immediately flashed back to the day before when I was driving Ivy home from school.

"Does this mean the Easter Bunny is canceling too?"

I dismissed that question as silly and told her not to worry about it. There in the store, I did. Easter for many children was a magical day, like with Santa. They were unable to grasp the religious meaning of it and instead basked in the wonders of waking up to gifts or treats.

Ivy was still in that mindset.

If things fell apart, would there ever be another Easter celebration? Would people who lost so much want to give into the yearly rituals that were created on days of faith? Would there be any faith in the world? I imagined the families of those eleven thousand in Houston were struggling with that.

Without thought, I grabbed candy, an item people were leaving alone.

"Clare, what are you doing? We don't need to waste money on that." He started pulling the items out of the cart.

"No, we do." I stopped him. "This could very well be the last Easter the world celebrates and I'll be damned if my daughter is going to miss it."

A simple nod of understanding from my father and he placed the candy back in the cart. All I had to do was mention Ivy's name to him, she was the light of his life. My father was the type of man motivated by the people in his life that he loved. Ours, not his life, was the reason behind the sudden shopping and ferry boat quarantine. Judging by the huge cart of items and the seriousness in my father's behavior, he was heavily motivated.

Five hundred and seventy-three dollars and four hours later, we headed back to Mills Run. While it seemed like a lot of money, in actuality, it probably would have cost a third before the virus rage. I believed we were stocked up. On the way home, we spoke about where we could 'park' the ferry, how we'd monitor the rest of the world to know when to come back, and start filling every container we could at home with water.

We had a plan and it felt good.

Self-quarantine meant staying away from everyone. I broke that rule the second we arrived in town and I saw Jael walking from the Quick Med.

"Can I stop and talk to him please?" I asked.

"Wear your mask. I'll see you at home."

I kissed my father on the cheek, placed on my mask and got out of the truck.

"Hey," I called out to Jael. "What's going on? You aren't sick are you?"

"No." He smiled and started walking with me. "Sam needed help getting things in order at the Quick Med."

"Does he have any new cases?"

Jael shook his head. "None. Yet. Human. There's been a few animal cases."

"We knew that was coming. How are you doing?"

He nodded. "Processing. Not really knowing what to do with myself. What are you doing out in the middle of the day?"

"Getting supplies with my father."

"For?"

"Hunkering down."

"Aw, you listened to Sam last night."

"Jael." I grabbed his arm and stopped him from walking. "You have been my friend since I got here. You were the only person who didn't treat me like a pity case because my husband died. You didn't treat me with kid glove care and for that I am forever grateful."

"Uh oh, where is this going?"

"We're taking the ferry down river and docking for a couple weeks until it blows over. I want you to go into self-quarantine for a few days, then come."

"Just leave town?"

"Yes. Leave. Stay alive. It's our best shot of beating this. Hide out until its run the course."

"I don't know, Clare. What if the town needs help?" Jael asked. "What if people get sick and need help?"

"What if you get sick and die? I want you with us and I need you with us. You have learned the ferry and my father and Michael can't be our only source of protection."

"I got news for you, Clare." He leaned down and winked. "You're a lot tougher than the whole lot of us."

I shrugged. "Probably. Still. Will you?"

"How long should I self-quarantine?"

"Three days. You can come to my house and wait with us."

He laughed. "No. You people are nuts. If I'm going spend three weeks sitting in the middle of the river with you, I'll need my space right now."

"So, you'll come?"

"I'll tell you what. I'll plan on coming. If this town needs me and I have to leave quarantine, then you go without me. Okay?"

"That works."

We parted ways and I reminded him as I left to get inside and stay there. I felt really positive about the plan, I did. As long as none of us got sick during the self-quarantine, we would be on the ferry and on our way. I was certain we were going to beat the virus that was kicking the world's ass.

SEVENTEEN – ONCE BITTEN

April 22

I dreamt of an Easter of the past; When the boys still believed a bunny brought them candy, when Ivy was too young to know and the candy my father force fed her was all over her new outfit.

It was a good dream and I believe I had it because I was in a good place when I went to bed.

The week in the house was trying. The recruiter kept reaching out to Michael, as if I would sign the papers to put him on volunteer duty. They needed people to help at medical camps that were being erected.

Absolutely not. He was needed at home.

Sam begged me to work at Quick Med. I couldn't. I had to worry about my family. As selfish as it was, my focus had to be my family. Mills Run wasn't over loaded with cases. There were eight of them, they died before the weekend. Again, the selfish person in me kicked in. I didn't want to know who they were. I had to keep my mindset on survival.

The day before we left was Easter Sunday and it was a good day. We shut off the phones, no television or internet. Although, I did allow Michael to talk to Sophia. Other than that, my mother made a ham and for a brief moment in time, everything seemed normal.

The world was falling apart, but my family was together and healthy. Michael was the only one of my children to know 'the plan'. I had to tell him because he wanted to know why I wouldn't let him go help out at medical camps.

He didn't get it.

I was being a mother. I was being selfish. I realized he wanted to help, I needed him to live.

What mother wouldn't make that same choice? Michael argued that it was like a war. Humanity versus a virus instead of a country and he was needed as a soldier.

Finally, using his analogy, I informed him our family was going AWOL. After some convincing, he accepted it. He helped his grandfather sneak our supplies on board the ferry. Two people approached them which reset our self-quarantine.

The last time we heard the news, multitudes of American cities were shutting down. No mass exoduses as people were too sick. Our part of the country was still operational, travel wasn't banned, but it was difficult. No one really traveled, there was nowhere to go. I suppose people were like us, hiding out in their homes or running to the hills. We'd all emerge when it was said and done.

We didn't wipe out all the food in the house. We were only going to be gone a few weeks, and when we got back we'd need supplies at the house. It wasn't barren, empty or void of food. It made it easy to tell Eli and Ivy we were just getting away for a few days.

Away from the craziness and the news of death.

I felt foreheads, checking everyone's temperature, annoyingly asking them again if they felt alright. They all did. Jael was already down on the Ferry, and I was making my last round to make sure we didn't leave anything we'd need.

We weren't coming back for weeks.

The can opener caught my attention, had it not been on the counter, I would have forgotten it. Not that my father wouldn't figure out how to open a can. I stuck it in my back pocket.

My mother pulled the blinds and then locked the front door. "Anything else?" she asked.

"No, I think we're good." I looked around the kitchen.

Eli walked up to me with Ivy. "Why can't we walk?"

"Because we're driving."

"It's only a couple of blocks," Eli said.

"I know. Do you have your charger?"

He nodded.

Ivy held up her book bag. "I got my dolls."

"Good. Good."

"Board games." Michael came into the kitchen. "We need these. I did a sweep. I think we got it all. Need me to do anything else?"

"No. I'm gonna walk through, go take the kids out with Gram. I'll be right there."

My mother and the kids shuffled out the door, it wasn't even twenty seconds later, I heard them arguing about getting in the car and who would sit where. Just as I turned my father walked back in.

"What's wrong?"

"I'm forgot the other rifle."

"Do we need it? I mean we have …" My eyes widened when I caught the sound of it.

"What is it?"

It was a familiar sound that I knew, that I would never forget. The sawing sound.

"Pap," Ivy called out. "Mr. Wester's dog is back."

"Something is wrong with it." Eli yelled.

"Shit!" I flew to the door. "Stay away from it," I hollered as I raced outside.

The moment my foot hit the back porch, everything unfolded in front of me in slow motion.

The SUV was only about fifteen feet away, yet it seemed like a mile.

Michael was at the back of the SUV holding Ivy's pink book bag, while my mother stood by the back door, with Eli and Ivy.

All of them focused on the Wester dog. A medium brown and gold terrier mix, was only a few feet from my mother, Eli and Ivy. It seemed to be leaning on its front paws, nose extended out while it's back hunched like a hyena waiting to attack.

It hacked and coughed, making that sawing noise.

The dog was sick and it eyed my family.

I wanted to shout again, however I was afraid of scaring the dog into reacting.

"No one move," I said softly. "Daddy?"

I heard the chamber engage on the pistol. "It's in my sight, Ivy is in the way."

Shit.

The dog hacked again, and this time it scared Ivy. She jerked and screamed in surprise and that was when it happened. Everyone saw it coming, everyone reacted.

The dog jumped.

Eli pulled at Ivy to bring her back as my mother reached out. I rushed from the porch at the same time Michael flew from the rear of the SUV.

We were all too slow.

With a snarling growl, the dog slammed into Ivy, knocking her back. She cried loud and shrill, but only for a moment. Michael arrived before me, swooping her pink book bag at the dog with a vengeance, sailing it into the dog and knocking him from Ivy.

The second I arrived, Michael had Ivy in his arms and was running into the house.

It was mayhem.

Ivy was crying hysterically.

"Put her on the counter," I ordered.

"Is she okay? Is she hurt?" My mother asked, frantically.

I didn't know. Ivy sat on the counter next to the sink. She cried out of control. I didn't know if she was hurt, scared or both.

"Eli, go to the bathroom, grab the antiseptic on the bottom shelf, hurry," I ordered and turned on the sink.

"Baby, calm down. Please." I told Ivy and yanked the roll of paper towels. A few sheets came loose and I ripped them off.

Like any six-year-old would do, she kept crying.

I extend the towels under the water. "I need to know …"

Bang.

Silence.

The gunshot caused me to jolt. I knew what it meant.

My father had killed the Wester dog.

It was like we were all put on pause. I stopped, the crying stopped, there was no noise. It was brief, then Ivy continued to cry.

"I need to know," I said to Ivy, wiping off her face. "Where are you hurt?"

She was too hysterical to answer.

My father hurried in. "Is she okay?"

"I'm trying to figure that out."

"Son of a bitch. That dog. I should have …"

"Dad." I stopped him, while visually checking my daughter.

"See if she's hurt. We need to know. Check. Look," my father said.

"I am. I am."

Ivy had fallen when the dog knocked into her. Was her head injured, her back? I looked for the source of what made her cry, feeling around, wiping that wad of wet paper towels over her, praying, *'please God, let her be fine.'*, all while hoping against all hope that the sick Wester dog didn't get her somehow.

"Here's the stuff," Eli said, holding the bottle to me.

"Thanks." I took it. "I don't think we need it."

"Yeah, she's bleeding," Eli said.

"Where?" I asked.

From his vantage point he saw it, where I could not.

He pointed and that was when I moved her long dark hair that draped over her shoulder.

My heart stopped beating. My entire world came crashing down, our escape plan came to a halt when I saw the blood on her neck.

Frantically, I poured the antiseptic on the paper towels and wiped the area.

Please, please, please, I begged in my mind.

I looked and wiped.

Nothing.

My legs weakened and my hands slammed to the counter, I nearly fell to the floor and had to catch my balance when I saw there wasn't a bite mark or scratch. The blood wasn't hers, it had to have come from the dog.

I grabbed on to Ivy and pulled her into my chest. "She's fine. She's not bit," I announced.

I heard the exhales of relief from everyone. The tension of those few minutes, dissipated.

Ivy still cried, even as I held her tight.

I couldn't give into the relief, I couldn't celebrate.

For as much as I wanted to believe that everything was going to be alright, I couldn't. Not yet. The truth was, the Wester dog may not have bitten Ivy, but he was sick and he came too close to my baby girl.

We weren't in the clear, not by a long shot. It was only matter of time before we knew if that virus we diligently fought to avoid, had found us after all.

EIGHTEEN – WAITING

We still wanted to take the ferry. The option was still on the table. Take our chances, pack up and go.

Was that fair to Jael? We were exposed. He wasn't.

After the Wester Dog incident, I called Sam right away. He stuttered some, probably not wanting to be truthful, then he was optimistic.

Although he was the one that put the final nail in the coffin about leaving on the ferry.

"You should stay near civilization," he said. "Just in case."

"In case one of us get sick? So, there's something that can be done."

"Not much. There have been maybe three cases that I heard of where the person beat the fever."

"Then why not leave?" I asked.

"Why not stay close to home? God forbid, one of you get sick, you should be home. Not floating down a river hundreds of miles away. If one of you get sick at the house then isolate. There are sheaths of plastic at the tent site outside the Quick Med."

"Seal off rooms?"

"Yes."

"Aren't you using those tents?" I asked.

"No, Clare, I examine the patient, give some relief medication and send them home. I go check on them there. It's for the best."

"How many people in town are sick now?"

"We've lost sixteen. About a hundred are in the throes of it."

A hundred? That many, it took my breath away.

"I suspect most of them will be gone by tomorrow," Sam said. "Then the next wave will hit."

"A hundred people, Sam?" I asked. "I mean, even sixteen is a lot. What do they do with the bodies? Where are they taking them? What about burials, funerals?"

"Conventional mourning has to be on hold now, Clare. It's a matter of public health. There are several funeral homes that are taking them for cremation. Feeny's is one. Don't you watch the news?"

"I avoided it, this weekend."

"Well, yesterday they announced that Jefferson County Health department will be using local sanitation companies to pick up bodies. I believe it's Tuesday, Thursday and Saturday. You have to mark the house with a yellow flag, make sure the body is identified, and place it outside.."

My gasp of shock and disgust cut him off. "Like trash. Jesus."

"It's either that or take the loved one to a crematorium, or to a mass burial site yourself. Which ironically are near the new med camps."

"Will it slow down?"

"Not before it gets worse. There are over a thousand people in this town. My guess in three or four days it will really hit big. That's what they're predicting for this area of the country. I'm going to try and drive up to Pittsburgh, maybe tomorrow before they close down and get medical supplies. It'll be a whole day trip. I have to though."

"What about Weirton, Wheeling or Steubenville? Can't you go there?"

"Too small. They can't spare any supplies," he said. "The medical camps went up today, and those aren't as big as Pittsburgh."

"What do we do? How long should we wait?"

"Two days. If in forty-eight hours no one is ill, then you are in the clear. You should get on your ferry and go."

"Will it work? I mean, what if we go, stay away, come back, aren't we coming back to danger."

"No," he replied. "The virus on the body dies about fifteen minutes after the body. On surfaces, twenty four hours tops. I said it before those who go in seclusion will survive. Once everyone who is to get sick, is sick, once it's done ... then the virus will die with everyone."

I listened to his words. I felt bad for Sam, handling everything himself. There was nothing I could do. I couldn't help. I had to think of my family. I told Jael that the trip was on hold two more days, I asked him to stay on the ferry and keep monitoring our radio. He would pick up things that we couldn't.

Sam ended the call telling me not to worry, but I did.

That dog coughed and hacked its sickness into the air around my children and my mother. The only ones not close enough were my father and myself.

We were back to reality in our own home, watching the news, or rather constant coverage of the virus. Most social media sites were down. The internet was spotty.

I tried again to get in contact with Trevor, he never responded. He hadn't in days, I could only think the worst. It wasn't like him not to respond.

I was worried sick and I prayed. I don't think I had prayed so hard since Jason got sick.

I even tried talking to Jason. If he had any pull whatsoever on the other side, the kids needed it. As if Jason was some heavenly being with powers.

With the state of the world, the way it was failing, again, for the first time in a long time, I started doubting the existence of the other side.

We were all walking on emotional egg shells. Any time someone coughed or sneezed, it was like a shock that caused us to instantly freeze.

A fearful shock. Was that the start?

The one that sneezed was just as scared as the rest of us.

I knew, as much as I hated it, I felt deep in my heart, we weren't in the clear at all. I was sick to my stomach because I knew that the next day one of us would be sick, I just didn't know who.

NINETEEN – ARRIVAL

April 23

As stubborn as I was, as hardheaded as I was, never in my life did I want to be more wrong. Unfortunately, I wasn't.

I was right.

I spent the evening pacing, trying to relieve my own fears, telling myself I was overreacting. From what I could find on the internet, I searched stories that debunked the animal to human transmission. I looked for survivor stories, anything with hope. Anything that would make me less crazy. I didn't know if it was intuition or paranoia.

The week prior, I was so focused on preparing to leave with my family that I shielded myself from reality. It was a conscious choice. I didn't want to concentrate on death and illness, I wanted to focus on life and surviving. It was a reality that hit me when I heard what sounded like the air brakes from a garbage truck just before dawn. Then I recalled what Sam had told me and what I saw reiterated on the local news. I didn't want to look out. I couldn't stop myself. It was Tuesday and a part of me knew what it was. Sure enough it was a garbage truck and it wasn't there to pick up refuse.

Two houses down at the Dawson's, the big green truck stopped and four men in hazmat suits emerged. They walked to the lawn and lifted the first body, it was big. Then they grabbed for another. My initial thought was the poor Dawson family had lost two members, there was only four of them. Until I saw the wrapped second body.

That one was small.

My heart beat hard against my chest. They had two children, ages nine and seven. I wondered which one died.

The house was dark except for a single blue glowing light. Probably the television. How horrible it had to be for the family, they were a good family. The parents were loving. It had to break their heart to place those who had died out on the curb like yesterday's trash. I know it broke mine for them. What choice did they have? No funeral home was picking up. They didn't have a car. They couldn't go to neighbors. I didn't even know they were sick. I was so self-absorbed, I didn't notice that my neighbors had bodies outside. That one of their precious children had succumbed to this brutal virus.

I watched until the truck pulled away.

It didn't help my restlessness.

The entire night before I barely slept, pushing myself to stay awake as if somehow, if I didn't sleep I would prevent the sickness from crossing into our threshold.

The fever virus was invisible to the naked eye, it was quiet and crept right in under my dutiful watch.

I dozed off for two hours and the second I woke up realizing I wasn't alone in bed, I knew who was sick.

Ivy was always the first one up. She thrived on being the early bird, sitting with my father, chatting away while he dipped Ritz crackers into his coffee.

Her breathing was heavy I could heard it clearly.

No, no, please, no.

Hesitantly I reached out to feel her. I didn't need to touch her to know that she was hot. I could smell the fever coming from her with each breath she released through her slightly parted lips.

My daughter's skin was hot and dry. I had never felt a fever so hot.

I whimpered as I scooted closer to her and pulled her near me. "Ivy. Ivy, baby." I gently shook her to get her to respond.

Ivy whimpered, with an airiness, spoke my name. "Mommy. Mommy, my head hurts."

As a mother who had nursed her children through many fevers, I knew that manner of speaking. I always called it fever talk. A child speaks softly, almost dazed, words more breath filled than strong.

Ivy spoke like that.

I wasn't thinking of myself, just of my sick baby girl. I pulled her to me and called out, "Dad! Dad!"

Ivy didn't jerk or move at my loud voice.

She barely responded.

No, it wasn't happening.

My father barreled into the room and I knew by the look on his face that I didn't need to say the words, "Ivy is sick."

"Oh my God." He stepped forward.

"Stop. Go check the boys. Check mom. Please."

He nodded and raced out of the room.

Who was I begging? God? My daughter? I just kept saying, 'please. No. Please. No.'

Holding Ivy, I grabbed my phone and dialed Sam.

It rang and rang. No answer.

"Sam, please answer." I tried again. Then I attempted to text him, but my fingers wouldn't work. I just put the word, "help' in there.

My father returned. "They're fine."

I exhaled in relief . My exhaling hurt every time I took a breath. Not my Ivy. Please not my baby.

My father tried, he really did try to be strong. I watched the muscles in his neck twitch as his face turned red and he stepped into the room.

"Daddy, no. Stay away."

"No." his voice cracked. "No, I'm not walking out of this room."

I rolled my daughter into my chest. "She's so hot. She's so fevered," I spoke while trying to control my tears. Then I saw them. My mother, Michael and Eli all rushed to the door way.

My father spun around. "Stay out of the room. All of you. Please," he said strong, then his voice quivered. "For the love of God, please."

"Mom?" Eli whimpered. "Please don't say Ivy is sick."

I closed my eyes tightly.

My mother moved to walk in.

"Melinda, stay back." My father held up his hand.

"John, that's my granddaughter."

"And those are our grandsons. Please. Just keep them away."

"I have to do something," she said.

Then it hit me. "Mom, run down to Quick Med. Sam isn't answering. Please, get him. Find him. Put a mask on."

"I'll go," Michael said.

"No. Don't go out there," I warned him.

"That's my baby sister. I can't stand by and do nothing. I'm going."

Before I could say anymore, Michael was gone.

My mother leaned against the doorframe, her hand to her mouth. Eli just stared. His brown eyes wide and a look of fear on his face.

"Take Eli downstairs, please, now," my father said softly, then reached out and closed the door.

"Daddy, please, don't, what are you doing?"

"If God intends for me to get this thing, I am going to get it whether or not I am in this room." He walked slowly to the bed. "I can't leave her. It's ... Ivy. It's my Ivy." He sat on the edge of the bed, then reached for my daughter and slipped his arms under her. I didn't want to let her go, but it was my father. He lifted her into his arms, her chest to his chest, and he cradled the back of her head in his hand, resting his cheek against her hair. "I'm here. Pappy is here. I'm right here baby," he whispered.

It hit me. He had been a part of every moment of Ivy's life since she was a baby. His heart was breaking as much as mine. While we both tried to be strong, it was impossible. I reached out and placed my head against his shoulder, my eyes kept looking to my phone.

Please, Sam, get back to me. Please.

I needed him to call.

My daughter, my baby girl was so sick and I just didn't know what to do.

TWENTY - OPTIONS

There is a sickening feeling that hits your gut and festers there when you find out that someone you love has an illness that could take their life. An immediate rapid progression through the five stages of grief hits before they step to the plate to take a swing at the fight.

When my husband, Jason was diagnosed, I went into denial, after all, he was young, why wouldn't he beat anything?

Ivy was young. That wasn't to her advantage. In her case, the five stages of grief mixed together to form one giant ball of angry sadness. I wanted to throw up and scream. If the virus was a physical entity I would have pulverized it. It wasn't fair, what had she done in her young life that she deserved to be so sick?

I wasn't fair to me, her family or to her … it wasn't fair to anyone who had the virus and who lost someone.

How did Mr. or Mrs. Dawson even handle it? I heard no cries of anguish coming from their home. Did they just surrender in defeat, hands up saying, "Okay, virus you won."

That wasn't me. It couldn't be me. It was my daughter and I would be damned if I would let her go quietly or without a fight.

It didn't help that Sam didn't answer. It made matter worse that Michael ran down to the Quick Med only to find a line of people waiting on Sam, with Jael at the door wearing a mask, taking names.

Why was Jael off the ferry? That angered me. Knowing my friend, he did it because people needed help. He put others first.

I was beside myself. My father and I took turns wiping Ivy down with a cool rag, nothing helped. We managed to get her to take a couple Tylenol, that didn't begin to touch the fever.

Finally, Sam returned my call. It wasn't really that long, it only seemed like forever, in reality it was only a couple hours.

"Clare, I'm sorry I missed your call. My phone died. I was getting supplies. What's going on?" he asked.

"It's Ivy. She's sick."

"I'll be right there."

He was.

Sam arrived, came into the bedroom and compassionately examined my daughter while my father and I stood by. He straightened the covers and ran his hand over her face when he was done. "She ... she has it."

I closed my eyes and wanted to collapse. My father grabbed onto me.

"Her lungs are not filling up, but the fever is taking a toll on her little body," Sam said. "I'm going to start IV fluids, that will keep her hydrated. I'll leave medication here. It will keep her comfortable and keep her from convulsing."

"Then what?" I asked.

Sam just looked at me.

"You said you went to get supplies. Is there something that can help her?"

"This is all I can do, Clare. Keep doing this, keep her comfortable until ..." He paused.

"No." I shook my head. "There has to be something that can be done."

"There isn't. You know this," he said. "I'm sorry."

"What if I took her to Steubenville, or Weirton, perhaps Pittsburgh?"

"Do you think they'll do more than I am doing?"

"Yes." I nodded. "Yes. Because you just give medication and send them home to die. It's easier than trying."

"Clare." My father snapped my name.

Sam held up his hand to my father. "I resent that Clare."

"I resent you giving up on my daughter."

"Clare, I swear to you, if I could come up with something, if there was anything I could give, Ivy would get it. I can't magically give something I don't have. There isn't anything. I'm so sorry."

"I'm sorry too. I can't give up." I walked around the bed, grabbing the throw blanket from the bottom.

"What are you doing?" Sam asked.

I pulled the covers down, covered Ivy with the throw and lifted her in my arms.

"Clare." My father grabbed my arm. "What are you doing?"

"I'm taking her to a hospital." I walked to the door.

"Hospitals aren't taking people," Sam said.

"Then I'll take her to a med camp. Maybe they can do something."

"They won't do any more than I am doing," Sam pleaded. "Please, I beg you. Don't. Don't take her there. They are finishing factories. Don't take her from her home, her bed, from surroundings she knows. Let her stay here and go from here in comfort."

He spoke the words, implying my daughter was going to die and they enraged me. I wanted to blast him. How dare him. "Fuck you, Sam. Fuck you." I reached for the door. "You said people beat this."

"They didn't have a magic pill. They just beat it. It's a one in a million shot."

"Well, my daughter is one in a million to me and I want that shot." I flung open the door, ignoring their pleas for me to stop. With Ivy in my arms, I barged down the stairs, instructed everyone to stay back, grabbed my purse and stormed out.

I didn't look at anyone or hear them, my focus was on getting Ivy help.

In my mind there had to be help out there. I just couldn't give up and not look.

After placing Ivy in the front seat of the truck, I got in, moved her to me, turned the ignition and holding on to her, I pulled out.

Driving down my street, I only paused a moment, and that was when I passed the Dawson's. I don't know why I did that.

On my lap, Ivy squirmed and moaned out, "Mommy."

"I'm here. I'm right here. Mommy's right here."

She whimpered in her illness and it caused my heart to hurt even more. I couldn't take away her pain or the fever that ravaged her, but I could try and fight it for her. I could try. That was all I could do.

TWENTY-ONE – SIGNAL

The moment I pulled from Mills Run, my phone rang nonstop. Beeps, blings and rings, it was unnerving. I was already emotionally out of control and not thinking clearly. Once on a bigger road, I hit 'answer' with the speaker.

"Come back, Clare," my father said. "Don't take her from us."

"I have to get her help."

"I realize that. I do. I know she is your daughter, but we all love her so much. I didn't get a chance to kiss her goodbye, to tell her I love her."

While he was on the phone with me, I heard the others.

"Mom, please come back with Ivy," Michael said.

"We need her here, Mom," said Eli. "I'll stay away, I promise. Please bring her home."

"Clare, sweetie, honey I know you're upset," added my mother.

"No one understands." I hung up.

I managed to drive maybe another mile, it had started to rain and I had to pull over to think. I realized it was my daughter and I was desperate for help, yet in my anguish, I was forgetting the others who loved and cared for her as much as I did. Was I being selfish? Was I wrong?

What parent wouldn't push the limits, take risks, if it meant saving their child, or at least trying?

I had to also think of my family. They weren't sick. I worried having Ivy around, would lessen their chances of staying healthy. Although I had heard on the news, pretty much most of the population was exposed or would be in the next several days, one way or another. Bottom line was, more than likely I was going to be sick in the next day or two. I needed my parents healthy for my boys.

Ivy stirred against me, groaning out a, "Pappy."

It made me want to cry. She needed my father, I didn't want to deny her of that, nor him of comforting her. What other choice did I have?

Then it hit me. I had a choice, there was a way.

After putting the truck in parking gear, I reached into my purse, grabbed my phone, checked my service, put it in the truck charger so as not to drain the battery, and hit the video call.

It rang several times, and then it connected. I could see the front porch of the house when my father answered, he went outside to take the call and I prayed the connection stayed.

"Clare," my father said.

"Hey, Dad, there's someone that wants you." I lowered the phone to Ivy and she lifted her head some.

"Pappy?" she called his name weakly.

"Hey sweetheart, how's my girl?" my father asked.

"Sick."

"Mommy's taking you to get you better."

"Is that Ivy?" Michael yelled and then his voice was closer. "Ivy, you get better. I love you."

"Ivy, when you come home, we'll play, okay," Eli said. "First you have to get better."

My mother joined in and they talked to Ivy. Elbow resting on the door of the truck, I covered my eyes with my hand, trying to catch the tears as my family encouraged her, wished her well and conveyed their love.

Ivy didn't answer much. She nodded, I could feel her doing that.

My father returned to the phone. "Ivy, Sweetheart, listen, Pappy needs you to get better. You do whatever they want you to do, okay? I love you very much. If you want me to be there, you tell Mommy and I'll be right there. You're Pappy's girl, you know that. I love you, baby, I love you so much."

"Love you too, pappy," her weak voice squeaked.

I reached for the phone. "Let me take that." Bringing it up, I wiped my eyes and sniffed.

"Thank you, Clare."

I nodded, "I'm sorry. I'm sorry I ran out. I'm so scared."

"I know. I know. We all are. You need … you need to be strong for her. Let her see how strong her mother is."

I nodded. "I'm trying."

"You're doing better than anyone could do."

"I'm going to see what they can do. If it isn't anything different than Sam could, then I'll be home. I have to try."

"I know you do."

"Watch my boys. Tell them I love them."

"We all love you. Keep me in the loop."

I peeped out an, "I will," told him that I loved him and ended the call. Placing the phone on the dashboard, I had to take a second and compose myself. There were so many tears dammed in my eyes, I could barely see.

For a moment. I sat there, hand on my daughter, listening to the soothing sound of rain beating against the truck and the wipers swishing back and forth.

Until the 'bang, bang, bang' on the window caused me to jolt.

I looked to the passenger's window. A woman about my age stood there, a blue hood covered her head and she was drenched.

"Can you help me?" she asked with desperation. "Please. My tire popped and I have no spare, my baby daughter is sick. Please help me."

Without thinking about it, I nodded. She darted away. Was there another car on the side of the road? I hadn't even noticed.

She returned and opened the door. She held a child wrapped in a blanket in her arms. The child wasn't an infant, maybe slightly smaller than Ivy. She called the child her 'baby' but then don't we all.

"Thank you. Thank you …" she paused and looked at Ivy. "Oh my God, I am so sorry."

"I'm sorry, too."

She awkwardly climbed in with the child, and I reached out to help her as much as I could. "I'm Diana," she said and closed the door.

"Clare."

She sniffed hard, it was obvious she was crying. "Thank you so much. I tried flagging cars. No one would stop. No one would help. I tried driving on the rim and then I saw you."

I put the truck in gear. "It's okay. We're all in the same boat."

"You wouldn't think so the way people are acting. No one cares. This is a child, who wouldn't help a child?" She cradled her child and kissed her. "It's okay, sweetie, we have help now. We're gonna get you to a doctor." She began to cry.

I flashed a sad smile to her as I pulled out onto the road. She mentioned the way people acted. Sadly, I was guilty of that. She may not have seen me differently because I allowed her in my truck. Truth was, I wouldn't have stopped for her. No, I didn't stop for her, because I remember seeing her and I just passed her by.

It was sad, I made the conscious decision right there as Diana wept in my car, no more. I was better than that. If a virus was dragging the human race down the tubes, I wasn't going to be one of those people to let humanity go with it.

TWENTY-TWO – BLUE BLANKET

There wasn't much conversation in the car. Her daughter was four and like, Ivy, woke up with a fever. Diana had lost her mother to the fever the day before. She herself wasn't looking well. I supposed that would be me in the next day or so. Other than the initial, 'this is my story' conversation, we spoke of how neither of us knew where the medical camp was located. I took Route 7 north to Steubenville. I was pretty certain Mingo Junction wouldn't have a medical camp, simply because Sam didn't mention it. It was a bigger small town than Mills Run, but it didn't operate on the small town mentality that we did, relying more on resources from its sister town, Steubenville. There were no signs, very little movement in the town until after we made our way through. It was a mere couple miles outside of our destination and as I neared Steubenville, there was slightly more cars on the road.

My first thought was to just go to the hospital, even though I knew they weren't taking people, maybe there would be some indication where the government camp was.

I was correct in my assumption, before we even arrived at the hospital, on the road leading to it, barricade horses blocked the road and two armed soldiers stood by.

I parked the truck where I knew I could turn around and told Diana, "I'll see if they know where to go."

She nodded. "I'll watch the girls."

I kissed Ivy, told her I'd be back. I don't believe she heard me.

The soldiers weren't interacting with each other, they stood a good fifteen feet apart, they were only enforcers and they wore masks.

"Excuse me," I said.

"Sorry, Ma'am, hospital isn't taking anyone."

"I know. I heard there's a medical set up. Do you know where?"

He replied, "It's located at the mall. Sporting goods store and super center parking lots."

"Thank you. Thank you so much." I knew where that was and how to get there. I turned around and hurried back to the truck, when I did, that's when I saw him.

I hadn't noticed him when I got out of the truck, perhaps because I was too focused. Yet, the older man, soaking wet, sat on the ground, a bright blue blanket, wrapped over him. His back was against the small wall and he looked at me as I walked by.

It made me pause and I back tracked. "Are you okay?"

He shook his head. His eyes were bloodshot, face pale, and a thin trickle of blood ran from his nostril across this lip. "No. I can't go any further. I walked here and … well."

I looked at him and all I could see was someone wrapped in some hideous eye screaming blanket, deathly sick, and drenched. This poor man, someone's father, grandfather, was probably going to die on the side of that road, twenty feet from soldiers who paid him no mind.

"I'm heading to the medical camp. Do you want a ride?" I asked him.

"If it's no bother."

"I don't have room in the truck. But if you want to ride in the back, there's a cover and it's dry."

"Thank you." He grunted, rolled to his side, placed his hand on the wall and struggled to stand. He stood a third of the way and fell back down.

There was no hesitation for me to help him, no fear of contagion. I had already signed my death warrant. I was in a closed in space with three sick people, and I had my daughter in my arms, my lips to her many times.

In my mind I was already infected, there was no way I wasn't.

My hand over the blue blanket, I walked him to the back of the truck, opened the gate and aided him inside. "I'm sorry you have to ride in the back."

He parted his cracked lips in an attempt to give a smile. "It's luxury, right now, thank you."

I closed the gate, got back in the truck and headed to the medical camp.

I took Sinclair Avenue to the mall. It was the way I knew. It was less residential and a faster route. As we neared the mall, a lane was block off and marked for 'Medical and Military personnel.' At the fork in the road, the right was shut down by military vehicles with access for designated workers and people. However, just after I made the left in the fork of the road, about a hundred feet from the super center driveway, everything stopped.

It was a massive parking lot. Cars and trucks on both sides of the road blocked the way. People just pulled up as far as they could and as close to the next car as they could and abandoned the vehicle. I didn't want to be one of those people.

Knowing that my plan was to leave if things didn't work out, I didn't want to be stuck. I backed up, turned the truck around, and parked way off the road where I believed I would be able to drive through the rough terrain and get back on Route Seven.

I made a mental note of the white rental moving truck not far from where I parked. I had a marker to find my way back.

We began our journey on foot, Ivy in my arms, her legs around my waist and head to my shoulder, Diana carried her child. Richard, as I learned his name was, tried his best to keep up. He moved slowly from the illness, we moved slowly from carrying children.

At the turn for the super center lot, I saw the reason for the backup. A lane was cleared and open and no vehicles were permitted in the lot.

The sounds of shouting, voices over PA systems and people crying carried to me before I even saw the camp.

We were about one of twenty heading to the camp. A huge dump truck honked its horn and we stepped to the side. When I did, I saw the back of the truck. It was filled with bodies. Why did I even look?

The medical camp was bigger than I imagined and less official than I anticipated.

There were only a few tents like the ones placed in front of the Quick Med, the rest looked more like party canopy's, the open sides were covered in clear plastic.

Everyone inside could be seen, the massive amounts of cots and people on them were overwhelming.

Once we got into the camp, I didn't have a clue where to go.

"Excuse me," I approached, what I believed was a worker in a hazmat suit. "Where do we ..."

"Areas are marked. Families are center tents. Solo adults to the right. Children left." He pointed. "Find a tent. Find a cot. Someone will be with you shortly."

I saw the first sign marked, "Children."

"This is where we part," Richard said. "Thank you."

"Good luck."

"Good luck to you and the little ones." He pulled that blue blanket tighter and walked in the other direction.

Diana and I with our daughters in arms, headed to find the children's area. I knew I had to hurry. Ivy was getting worse, her little legs lost their grip around me.

It took us five tents to find one with an open cot. Actually Diana found one first, she offered it to me because I helped her. I declined and in the next tent I found an available space for my daughter.

The cot was small, almost designed for a child, it had an IV pole attached with a folded blanket on the foot and a pillow that resembled something you'd get on an airplane.

My regrets for bringing her to the camp didn't start right away, in fact I was grateful. I hadn't even set her down, when a woman wearing a less scary version of a hazmat suit approached.

She introduced herself as doctor so and so, I didn't hear it, or wasn't paying close enough attention. She asked me to place Ivy on the cot. The first thing she did was run a forehead thermometer over her head, then she examined her.

"How long has she been symptomatic?" she asked.

I looked at my watch. "Five hours. I woke up at nine and she was like this. I went to bed around six am and she was fine."

"Ivy," the doctor said her name. "Ivy?"

My daughter didn't respond.

"When did she stop responding?"

"Not long ago. She's been moaning and fidgeting, I think she's just sleeping."

The doctor lifted her eyelid, pulled out a flashlight pen and shined it in her eye, then checked the other. After that, she continued the exam.

"Her lungs are clear, but you know her fever is very high, right?"

"I do."

A male worker approached, dressed similarly, he handed the doctor a clipboard and hung an IV bag on the pole. She wrote something and handed the board back to the male.

"My name is Mark, Ivy, right?" he asked, placed the board on the cot, then lifted Ivy's wrists and placed a band over her. "She's tiny. Poor little baby." He was so compassionate, gently running his gloved fingers across her forehead, clearing her hair. It took a while for him to find a viable vein, but he managed to get one in her foot.

I watched him inject something into the IV. "What is that?" I asked.

"It's a mixture of analgesic and antipyretic. It will ease her headache and cull the fever some." He was a complete contrast to the doctor. She was cool in her approach, although she would have to be.

Mark covered Ivy and said he'd be back.

Ivy hadn't responded, she was in some sort of deep sleep. I kissed her forehead; it was so hot. I decided to send my father a text, letting him know we had arrived and Ivy was getting treatment. It was all I could tell him, other than the entire place was packed.

When I set down my phone, I looked at Ivy's band. Her name was handwritten and next to it was a number. 7564.

A twinge of fear hit me. I hoped to God she wasn't patient number 7564, not with only eleven thousand people in Steubenville. Then I looked around in the tent. It was the first time I had really done so. It was a full tent, more than a hundred beds filled with children. Some had parents with them, some did not. It was one tent of many. All my flip flopping, all the back and forth, the virus wasn't real, it was real, all that ended right there and then. Not only did I see the magnitude of it in that tent, I felt and saw it with my own daughter.

There would be no more flipping.

This was bigger than the Spanish flu, the Bubonic Plague and the Justinian Plague, this thing… this fever was it, the big one.

Mankind was mere markings on a whiteboard and Mother Nature found a way to erase us all.

<><><><>

Mark brought me a chair after about an hour and a cup of soup. I wasn't hungry, but he told me to eat something to keep up my strength to fight the virus myself.

That made me laugh internally. Who was he kidding? I was surrounded by it. My days were numbered and that made me sad. Not that I was going to get sick. , but to think of my boys. At least they had my father and mother.

I was impressed at how things were run. For as busy as they were, someone came by and checked on Ivy regularly. The same exam, temperature, heart, lungs and eyes, then they'd make a notation on the chart.

I talked to Ivy a lot, whispering in her ear. I even had my father talk to her.

She didn't move, or wake up.

Mark came back in four hours and changed her IV, gave her more medication. I thought about Diana and wondered how her daughter was. I also thought about how I reacted to Sam, how mean and angry I was with him.

During the time I sat there, I watched them carry out at least a dozen children. It was incredibly sad and hard to see. Watching them take the child, hearing the horrifying cries of pain from the parent.

"That won't be you," I'd whisper in Ivy's ear. "Not you."

There was one woman who stood by a cot a row over. Several times during the day we made eye contact. She was nurturing and caring to her child, but she was calm. With each passing hour, I could see how pale she grew. She was obviously ill.

When they covered her son and pronounced him as gone, her reaction was different. She didn't cry out or react. She nodded her understanding, kissed her child once and allowed them to take him. Her hand stayed on her boy until they took him too far away.

She gathered her things, tossed a purse over her shoulder and turned. Then she stopped and walked over to me.

"I just wanted to wish you the best," she said.

"Thank you," I said. "I am so sorry for you loss."

"Me, too. Danny was my fourth child that I lost."

"Oh my God." I couldn't even process what she said. "I'm sorry."

"It doesn't get any easier, it just absorbed into the numb and pain that's already there. You know?" She sniffed. "I better be going. I'll pray for you. I mean that, too. I will pray."

"Thank you."

She turned and began to leave. She lost her balance once, she was weak. I wondered if she was going home or maybe to a tent to rest.

Then not long after the woman had left, more children were removed, the onset of regret began when the second IV bad was empty.

I hadn't seen Mark or any other worker come over. I thought maybe they were going to finally give her another bag instead they removed the line completely.

"Wait," I called out. "When are you coming back?"

No answer.

I began to panic. I lifted my phone, almost instinctively to call the life line I always took for granted and noticed I was down to ten percent battery. Plus, I couldn't call Sam, I had lost that privilege, so I placed the phone back in my jacket pocket.

Finally, I spotted her. That same doctor from earlier in the day. I called out to her maybe three times before she acknowledged me and came over.

"They took away her IV out," I said, panicked.

"Yes."

"Is she not getting another?"

"Ma'am," the doctor spoke softly. "Your daughter's temperature has not dropped below 106 all day, in fact it has been 107. Do you understand what that means?"

"What about the medicine?"

"It's treatment, to make her comfortable. Her fever has been constant at 107."

I snapped my words. "Okay you said that. It's high that's why she needs more."

"No, she doesn't," the doctor said gently. "Her pupils are not responding. She ... is not responding."

"She's alive."

"Yes, but unfortunately, the fever has caused brain damage and we can't spare the resources on her. She won't make it through the night."

Slam!

I felt as if I were hit in the chest with a baseball bat.

"I'm sorry." She walked away.

She was sorry? Why was I there all day? Why didn't anyone tell me how bad her fever was?

I couldn't move, my body trembled, my face felt flush and I looked down to Ivy.

My child was dying.

Why did I take her from her family? Why didn't I believe Sam? There I was surrounded by strangers in a god forsaken tent, miles from home.

I did exactly as Sam said I would. I robbed my child from being at home and surrounded by those she loved. Her last lucid moments were spent on my lap in a pickup truck.

I couldn't change what I had done, instead I could change how it all ended.

Keeping Ivy covered, I lifted her from the cot. Her arms dropped to her sides, I lifted them and rolled her into my chest.

My focus now was to take her home.

Leave the tent, the camp and get to my truck.

I walked out and nearly to the end of the camp a truck rolled by me. It was packed with bodies. I wouldn't have looked away had I not spotted it. That hideous bright blue blanket that Richard wore. It was wrapped around a body. Richard had died.

Fueled by emotion, I moved faster.

"We're going home, Ivy, we're going home," I kept telling her.

If it were the last thing I did, I was going to make sure my daughter did not leave the earth in the middle of some medical camp. She was not going to just be number 7564 and dumped in the back of a truck.

After spotting that moving truck, I found my own, just where I put it in the side of the road. Things had gotten worse. I was no longer parked near the end of the cars, I was so far in the middle, there was no way to get out or around. As far as I could see in the darkness were cars, packed in tightly. I didn't have a clue how far they extended.

All of my efforts were futile. I had failed my family and my child.

TWENTY-THREE – CLUTCH

April 24

The desperation and loss I felt surrounded by a sea of cars was immeasurable. Ivy tight to my chest, I crumbled physically to the ground and moaned my lowest form of defeat.

I sobbed out, totally lost on what to do. "I'm sorry, Ivy. I am so sorry."

How was I going to get home? Get anywhere for that matter. I was in the same position as Richard when I spotted him. Lost on the side of the road.

The vibration coming from my pocket, immediately flipped a switch. My phone wasn't dead. Hurriedly, I reached for it and pulled it out.

It was my father.

"Daddy," I said his name with sobbing breaths.

"No, don't tell me…"

"We're here. She's not gonna make it. She's not gonna make it through the night and I …wanted to bring her home…" My words got lost in hyperventilated breaths.

"Clare, calm down. Are you still at the camp?"

"No. I started to leave. The truck is blocked in. There are so many cars."

"Where? Where are you?" he asked.

"Sinclair Ave. It's all cars."

"Listen to me. Make your way as far as you can. I'm on my way. I'll be there."

"Please, hurry, she isn't …"

Beep. Beep. Beep.

My phone died.

I wanted to throw it, somehow I stopped myself. I grasped it tight, then shoved it in my pocket. I was so scared. No connection, no line to my father, how would I find him? How would I know when he arrived? He said to go as far as I could so I would do that.

Saying a prayer, I checked my daughter to make sure she was still breathing. I could feel the heat from her body against mine, and using all my strength, I stood.

"Pappy's coming. He's coming. He'll be here. Please hold on."

Mills Run wasn't that far. On good traffic days I made it to Steubenville in twenty minutes. My father wouldn't take long. He had to find us and we had to find him.

I began my journey through the cars. It was dark and impossible to see, I didn't even know how far I would have to walk. I just knew it seemed endless. People who were sick, or carrying ill walked by me. How many would come?

Despite becoming winded by not only moving and carrying Ivy, I kept talking to her. Hoping she would hear every word I said. I regretted every moment I didn't grasp with her. Every single time I told her "Not right now. Later." It should have been, "Right Now." I never realized one day there wouldn't be a "Later" day. It came sooner than I could of ever imagined.

The maze of cars seemed to grow. I was like a nomad wandering aimlessly, ignoring people who called out to me, asking me if the medical camp was ahead.

I just needed my father and at the rate I was going, I thought that was impossible.

Until through the darkness, I heard the call of my name.

"Clare! Clare where are you?"

I wheezed out an emotional groan of relief and then with everything I had I screamed out, "Dad! Dad!"

"Stay put, just call out my name."

I leaned against the next car I came to and hollered his name a good four times. Then I saw him.

My father had always been my hero and at that moment, he truly was. I tried my hardest not to cry. When he saw us, he raced our way and took us both in his arms.

"I didn't know what to do." I cried against his shoulder.

"It's okay. Let's go."

I nodded.

"Let me take her."

I surrendered Ivy to him, the moment he took her into the folds of his arms my father released this moan of pain that moved like a dagger into my soul.

He was broken.

His heart crushed before me and I saw it. I felt it.

Placing his lips to Ivy, he brought her close to his chest. "I'm here. Pappy's here. Let's go home." His voice quivered. "Let's go home."

I don't know how far we walked. I stayed close to my father who barely looked ahead. He kept staring down to Ivy.

We kept walking by people trying to get to the medical camp. It wasn't stopping. I knew this virus would not stop until it was completely done, taking everyone in its path.

It didn't take long to get to the end of the line of cars where my father had parked. I was so happy to see his SUV.

"Traffic isn't bad. There's none," he said when we arrived. "We'll be home before long."

I opened the back door, got inside and he placed Ivy in my arms.

I brought my nose close to her lips, trying to breathe in her exhales, feeling the heat, feeling what was left of her life.

There was no doubt in my mind that it wouldn't take long to get home. My father drove top speed. I didn't believe the short span of time it took to get there wouldn't be enough.

Then again, there was never going to be enough time.

I felt it happen sometime after we crossed into Mills Run.

I knew because I was watching her.

Ivy's eyes opened and she looked at me. She looked at me and then ... she was gone.

There was no fanfare, no grand goodbye, no last "Mommy, I love you." There was nothing but silence and one final look as my baby girl left this earth while in my arms.

I froze. It was almost instantly, her fevered body started to cool as we pulled into the driveway.

"We're here," my father said. "We'll get her inside and call Sam."

I believe I didn't even blink. I was in a momentary state of shock.

"Clare?"

I shivered a breath as I inhaled through my sluggish nostrils.

"Clare?"

I lifted my head and my eyes met his in the rearview mirror.

He knew. "No," he said softly. "No."

I felt it build. It stirred in my gut, ripped through my heart and escaped from my throat as a long, building deep scream.

My father's head dropped forward to the steering wheel as he gripped it.

I couldn't stop screaming. A crying scream that was beyond my control. I clutched Ivy to my chest tightly, holding her against me as if I were trying to bring her in, give her my life, be a compression against my bleeding, broken heart.

Nothing would work.

The pain was immediate and unbearable.

Ivy was gone.

Gone.

Not one thing was going to take away the pain of losing my child, and nothing ... was ever going to bring her back.

TWENTY-THREE - PICK UP SHEET

Physically I couldn't move. Emotionally, I didn't want to. I didn't know what the next day or even the next several hours would bring, but I wasn't ready to let go of Ivy.

Not yet.

After my meltdown in the car, and I suppose after my father's quiet meltdown, there was silence and then he spoke.

"We should go inside now," he said. "Sam said there's no risk of infection after …" he coughed on his emotions. "After."

"I just need a moment, please," I said dazed.

"Absolutely." He opened the car door and paused. "Clare, I am so sorry."

"I am too. Thank you for bringing us home."

He cleared his throat and then stepped out.

I really needed a moment.

There in the back seat, I stared forward just holding my daughter. I went through bouts of shocked silence and crying. They traded off.

Even though I knew I had to go into the house, I couldn't move. I didn't sleep, I did nothing but stay in the back seat. I thought of the past, all the times we had with our family. I took a small amount of comfort in the fact that, should there be a heaven, Jason was waiting on our daughter.

The sun came up and I still stayed there. I didn't have a clue what time it was, my eyes were locked forward, focusing on nothing while I held Ivy.

Then there was a knock on the door and it opened.

Sam was there, wearing his mask. "Clare."

I shifted my eyes only briefly to him then resumed staring forward.

"I know I'm not your favorite person right now," he said. "But I …"

"Are my boys okay?"

"Yes."

"My parents?"

"Yes."

"Thank you."

"Clare." He placed his hand on my arm. "Everyone needs you to go in. They need to say their goodbyes to Ivy."

I blinked and held my eyes closed for a moment. "Then what?"

"Excuse me? What do you mean?"

"They say goodbyes, then what? Wasn't it you who said conventional mourning is done."

"I did."

"What can I do?" I asked. "What do I do with my daughter. I can't ... I can't take her back to the camp. They don't care about the dead. They just toss them. I can't put her out like trash."

"Listen, I am going to be one hundred percent honest with you, okay? A couple more days, that will be the only option. Mass graves, or bury the loved ones yourself."

"Is that what I do, Sam? Dig a hole in the backyard. She deserves better."

"Everyone deserves better, but that's not the way it's going to be. My own father .... He died last night, Clare. I'm ... I'm heading to Feeny's this afternoon to say my goodbye."

I shifted my eyes to him. "Your father died?"

He nodded.

"I'm sorry, Sam."

"I am too. I'm sorry about Ivy. Come with me. We'll take Ivy there. At least in a few days, you can have something of her."

"Her ashes."

"Yes."

I inhaled deeply.

"They won't take people for long," Sam said. "Mr. Feeny picked up my father as a favor. They aren't picking up anyone anymore and are overrun. Take this ride with me."

"Is it the right thing to do?"

"Clare, what choice is there? This is horrible, this is not the way we want to say goodbye, but this is it. Now, please, let your family have their last moments with Ivy."

"Okay. Just a few more minutes."

"You've been out here ten hours."

In shock I looked at him. 'That long?"

He nodded.

"Why am I not sick?"

"I don't know."

"I should be sick. Within twenty four hours, right? I'm not sick."

"Your dad isn't either. He should be as well. We don't know. Just give me Ivy and let's go into the house. One step at a time. One day at a time."

Had he not told me how long I was in the backseat, I wouldn't have known. I looked out the window and my entire family, battered with grief, were standing on the porch.

I had my time with Ivy. They deserved theirs.

I nodded to Sam, allowing him to lift Ivy. He carried her from the SUV, yet I stayed. I had finally stopped crying for the time being. I wasn't ready to break down again, and I knew I would when I looked at them.

I wasn't ready to do anything. I couldn't even get out of the car and deal with what needed to be done for Ivy, nor face what would come in the next few days.

As a strong woman, I knew I could take the time I needed, but soon enough I would have to pull it together. Not for me, for my sons. I may had lost a daughter, however they still had a mother and they needed me.

It was a hard resolution, but I reached it. I would take the ride with Sam to Feeny's in Weirton and entrust them with my precious asset. Jael came to the house to pay his respects, express his sympathy and say he was sorry.

The word sorry was used so much by everyone, I wondered when it would lose its impact.

I gave my family time alone with Ivy since they hadn't seen her. I stayed outside, watching the Dawson home and talking to Jael when he arrived.

When I went inside I believed my mother had some sort of mental breakdown. I asked where Ivy was and my father pointed upwards.

She had Ivy on the bed, covered from the waist down with a pink crocheted lap blanket. Not only had my mother changed Ivy's clothes, but she sat on the bed next to my daughter's. Ivy's face had discolored from where the blood had polled when I held her against me and my mother was applying makeup.

"Mom?"

She sniffled. "I wish I had spent more time with her."

"You are a great grandmother. She knew you loved her."

"Yeah, I know,"

"Can I ask what you're doing?"

"Did you know I went to school to be a beautician?" she asked. "Instead of practicing in a salon, I worked at a funeral home. Part of the makeup, the clothing, everything, it's done so when we say goodbye, we remember the person as they were." She closed the compact and set it on the nightstand. "She's so beautiful."

Maybe she sensed my uncomfortableness with what she had done. It made me feel strange. Then I looked at my daughter.

The blue tint to her skin was gone, as were the dark black spot on the side of her face. She looked peaceful.

"I wanted everyone to have this last look. Let's get everyone, say a prayer and you can carry her out as if she is sleeping."

She left to get my father and boys. A part of me thought it was morbid what my mother had done. I then remembered before there were funeral homes, before our modern rituals, people grieved and mourned differently. They had placed loved ones in chairs, even in beds and took photographs.

Sam said we had to forego the process we all had become accustomed to.

Despite my initial reluctance to accept what my mother had done, to appreciate it, I knew she was trying to do something. That something was far better than handing Ivy to a dump truck, or wrapping her in a shower curtain and putting her on the curb.

<><><><>

Sam didn't even know his father was sick. Those who worked with him did. They told Sam his father never stopped, he kept going, even though he grew desperately ill. He sat down to take a break and he died.

He told me the story on the way to Feeny's.

It wasn't a long drive, but getting close to Feeny's was nearly impossible. The small lot was filled and there wasn't a space on the street.

Finally, Sam dropped us off at the front and went to look for a spot. I was told to bring a container for the ashes and a photograph since I didn't have identification for Ivy.

I felt horrible. All I had was a mason jar with a flip lock lid, it was stuffed in my purse as I walked the path to the front.

It was obvious Feeny's had perfected their system. I could see people walking to the side door, and those leaving carried jars, small boxes, items I assumed contained the remains of those they lost.

I wasn't the only one who heard about Feeny's. There were at least ten people ahead of me, some held children in their arms, others used blankets as a make shift gurney. There was a wait to get in the door.

Once inside, there was an older man with a clipboard, he took my name, Ivy's name and other information. He handed me the paper. "Here you go, dear. Take Ivy back to the Palmer room. Someone will be with you. They'll give you the bottom half of that sheet. You'll need that when you come back for Ivy. I'm very sorry for your loss."

There was that word again. Sorry. I wondered how many times a day he said it and did he even mean it?

Feeny's was a bigger funeral home with six viewing rooms. I had to find the Palmer room, which was far in the back.

There was a short line at the door. The three men before me had children in their arms. At the door was a priest, I watched his lips move as he motioned his hand over the deceased child, then he blessed himself.

I stayed back and added distance to give each of them privacy.

When I approached, there wasn't a question if I wanted a blessing. I stopped before the priest.

"Child's name?" he asked.

"Ivy."

He held a tiny container in his hand, placed in his thumb then touched Ivy's forehead.

Moving his hand in the sign of the cross, he said, "Eternal rest grant unto her oh Lord and..."

"And let your perpetual light shine upon her," I said with him.

"May Ivy rest in peace. Amen."

"Amen. Thank you, Father."

His lips pursed in a sad smile and I walked into the large room.

I didn't know what to expect, but I was certain, it wasn't what I saw.

The room was filled with tables and on them were children, all children. The temperature was extremely cold yet a soft, happier music played over a speaker.

Parents placed their child down, a tired looking worker came over, spoke to them a moment, and with their half sheet of pink paper, they sadly walked out, leaving their loved one behind.

A drop off.

A gentle and compassionate one. Feeny's was doing their best to accommodate and help. It was just so hard to do. How does one just leave their child behind? I felt guilty doing so and I had to keep reminding myself that it wasn't Ivy anymore, my Ivy was gone.

They promised they'd be gentle and take good care of her. I was to come back any time after the end of the week and she'd be ready.

Using Sam as my excuse and waiting on him, I stayed longer than everyone else did to drop off their child. No one rushed me or said anything.

Eventually, I did walk away. Broken hearted, feeling guilty and again crying. It was an incredibly difficult thing to do. I knew it was just another hard step in the road that wasn't going to get easier any time soon.

◇◇◇◇

My phone had been dead for a while and I worried it wouldn't come back to life. I charged it in Sam's car and it had some juice when we left Feeny's. I was worried about the boys and my parents. I called as soon as I could.

"How did everything go?" my father asked.

"It went okay. As well as can be expected. Are the boys alright? Mom? You?"

"We're fine. None of us are sick. I'm thinking maybe we should reset that self-quarantine again. I've been staying pretty clear of people as best as I can."

After a few more words, I ended the call with my father and gave heavy thought to what he had said about resetting our family self-quarantine.

I didn't think that would work for me. I honestly, one hundred percent believed that I was going to get the virus. It was something I could 'See' happening and it wasn't a matter of if, it was a matter of when.

My sons were a different story. I didn't know if they were going to get sick, all I knew is that I had to prevent it.

The quarantining and leaving was a way to ensure that. My mind was almost made up when we drove past the Weirton Quick Med. There was a line out the door and people were camping in the lot as if some sort of miracle was going to be delivered to them at the fast food place of medical care.

"How many people work there?" I asked Sam.

"Three at peak times. Nurse practitioner and my father was there. That's where he died."

"And they're still working?"

"Yes, they are."

"Is it the right thing to do?" I asked. "I mean if you're healthy enough to help, should you?"

"There's no right or wrong on this. You do what you need to do. I look it at personally as if I needed help and someone just walked by me, how would I feel?'

His words reminded me of Diana and how others and myself drove by her without a second thought. How I made a promise to myself that I wouldn't do that again.

There was a lot more help needed than just giving out an aspirin and fluids, there was the aftermath as well for those who were still standing.

Leaving, hiding and staying away wasn't wrong, it just wasn't the humane thing to do.

If we wanted humanity to survive, then we had to be humane.

Were we obligated as a species to be there for one another? I wrestled with those thoughts on the way home only briefly. I knew what I was going to do. Because, albeit not for long, I was still standing and strong.

TWENTY-FOUR – KEEP GOING

Even though Sam claimed he wasn't an alcoholic, I knew better. He didn't drink all day, in fact he had a strict rule to only drink after dark unless he was stressed. He was what I would call a functioning alcoholic. He added proof to that when he popped open the glove department and handed me a soda bottle full of vodka.

I had a drink, then so did he. The situation warranted it. In a sense I buried my daughter and he buried his father.

The roads were eerily clear and we put on the radio to listen to the local news. Reports out of Pittsburgh weren't good. The medical camps were overrun and they were putting medicine distribution on a schedule.

Most of the western United States had been silent. No news reports at all. Not even on the few sites that remained on the internet said anything about the west.

There was still an internet connection, electricity, running water and cell service, but local experts were predicting they would probably go down before the end of the month.

All essential services would probably be done within a week.

We had been stockpiling water for days and storing it on the ferry, which had its own water supply. I wasn't sure how many thousands of gallons, it didn't matter. We all made fun of my father when he bought a reverse osmosis water maker.

I wasn't laughing anymore.

Mills Run was a tight community, I trusted everything on the ferry was safe. We were pretty hidden and I didn't worry too much about anyone coming and taking it.

Since the animal control ordinance the streets had been pretty empty. On this day, though, people were in front of the Quick Med. Many people.

Sam exhaled. "This is going to be a long day." He stared outward to the Quick Med. "So many people and I'm not even counting the ones at home. They need checked on, also."

"Do you need help?" I asked.

Sam literally did a double take. He looked at me, then to the Quick Med, then back to me. "I wouldn't ask you that."

"You're not asking. I'm offering."

"No, you and your family. You need to restart the self-quarantine."

"Sam," I said his name softly. "Let's be real here, okay? I held Ivy, kissed her, was in a closed in space with her. I picked up a woman who had a sick child, she was sick. I helped a dying man into the truck and I sat in a tent full of infected. I'm not walking away from this. No amount of self-quarantine is going to help me. By tomorrow I'll be done, so let me help you today."

"Clare, your family ...."

"The best I can do for them is keep a distance. Keep in contact while keeping a distance. My father is doing the same. I'll do it, because right now my boys are fine. They ..." I paused and hurriedly looked at Sam. "They're fine."

"Yes. That's why they need to be quarantined."

"They do." I grabbed the door handle. "Let me tell them I am helping you today and I'll be back. First I have to find Jael. See you in a bit." I stepped out and closed the door.

Sam had parked a block from the Quick Med. I could see the ferry and I headed in that direction.

"Clare!" Sam called me. "Where are you going?"

I pointed to the ferry. "To see Jael."

"He's not there."

I turned around. "Where is he?"

Sam pointed. Jael wore a round mask and one of those paper hazmat suits that remained from the CDC tents. He stood outside the Quick Med with a clipboard, and it looked like he was writing down names.

"Damn it." I charged that way, calling out his name until I caught his attention. Keeping my distance, I waved him to me and waited until he came over. He took his time.

"Are you okay?" he asked, softly. "Something wrong?"

"Jael, when you came to the house, I kept my distance. I told you to get on the ferry."

"I told you that I would only do that if my help wasn't needed. It was needed. Take a look."

"I need you. Have you been keeping yourself protected?"

"Yes, but Clare..."

"Good. I'll take over. I've been exposed," I said.

"Clare..."

"I need you to get to the ferry. I want you to get my sons and take them. Take them down river and wait..."

"Clare..." he tried to interrupt again.

"Two or three weeks. Monitor the radio system. Come back early only if God forbid, someone gets sick. If not, don't come back until ..."

"Clare," Jael said my name firm. "I can't do that."

"You know how to man the ferry."

Jael nodded. "I do. That's not why. I've been around the sick."

"You're wearing protective garb.

"I am. But ... yesterday, Mrs. Dawson needed ..." he grunted. "This protection ..." He pointed to the mask. "It's more for them, than me."

I tilted my head with question and that was when I noticed. His eyes were blood shot and the area around them dark.

"Jael?"

He lowered his face mask. His usually tan complexion was pale and blotchy. His lips were swollen and there was a twinge of blood around his nostril.

"I'm sorry, Clare," he said. "I'm already sick."

TWENTY-FIVE - EVERYTHING CHANGES

Not Jael.

He was my first and only friend when I moved to Mills Run and he was sick. I begged him to stop, that I would take over, but he wouldn't. After telling Sam that Jael had the fever, he gave him an injection that would help lower his temperature and ease his headache.

I wanted to help Sam, do my part and take my mind off of Ivy, although that would never really happen. At least it would make me stop obsessing about my sons. The number one thing I needed to do was not become that person who wanted to curl up and die. Like I had done with Jason. My children needed me, my parents and the community needed me.

After trying to get Jael to take a break, I needed to tell my family what I was doing and let them know I was back from Feeny's. I walked to my home thinking about Ivy, how I left her there. I had to keep telling myself she didn't know. She wasn't lonely or scared.

Walking those blocks to my house, I also thought of Jael. Maybe he would be that one in a million that recovered, I hoped so. No, I hoped everyone defied the odds. In my fantasy world, the fever suddenly stopped being deadly.

It mutated constantly according to Sam, so why couldn't it mutate for the better?

Perhaps that was my ignorance on viruses showing through.

When I arrived at my home, my father was on the front porch. He was just sitting there and out front on the lawn was the four person tent.

"Hey," he stood when he saw me. "You're back. How are you?"

I nodded. "Doing. It was hard."

"I can only imagine."

"What uh ..." I pointed to the tent.

"You and I ... we're on quarantine. We were both too close to it and exposed. I still believe if we're meant to get it, we will. If not, we won't. I'm not taking a chance with them. They ..." He pointed to the house. "Are also on quarantine. They're not allowed out. It has been tough with Michael. He wants to see Sophia. They understand though."

"So we're outside, huh? I'm uh ... I decided to help Sam."

"At the Quick Med?"

"Actually, he wants me to start canvassing the town since I know it and all the people here. See whose car is gone, who is sick, who has a body out. Do my part, you know, until I come down with it."

"You may not."

I chuckled emotionally. "I will. I've had more exposure than most people. I'll get it." I folded my arms tight to my body. "Jael is sick."

My father titled his head. "Aw, no. really?"

"Yeah. He's down there helping. I'm here to tell the boys and mom, then head back down. So, I won't be keeping you company out here on the lawn."

"How about I keep you company down there and I help out as well."

"Are you sure?"

My father nodded. "Yeah, I'd like to do that. Been here long enough and those people are family, too."

"Sam needs help. Thank you."

"Plus, it will stop me from sitting here and thinking about my Ivy."

"No, no it won't. You will just keep moving and doing while thinking about her. How do I uh ..." I indicated to the house.

"Knock on the window. They know not to come out."

I stepped on the porch and moved to the front window, then knocked.

Eli appeared in seconds. My poor son looked so sad. His hand touched on the window.

"Hey, Mom."

"Hey, Sweetie."

"You sick?" he asked.

I shook my head. "Not yet."

"How was Ivy?"

I didn't even know how to answer that question. I shrugged and shook my head and was so glad when Michael and my mother arrived at the window.

In my entire life, I never saw my mother not looking her best. Yet in her defense, she hadn't a stitch of make up on, nor her signature lipstick. Her hair was pulled back.

"Dad said we can't come out or near you," My mother told me.

"That's for the best," I said.

"Pap won't let me go see Sophia," Michael said.

"That also is for the best. Look ... I know this is tough, here's what I need from you. In two days, should all of you still be healthy, I want you three on the ferry. You don't need to go anywhere, it's already far enough away from everything. You go there and wait it out. Michael, if Sophia and her family are fine, you invite them along, Okay?"

"Yeah." He nodded. "They locked themselves in their house. They need food mom, that's why I want to go over."

"I'll tell you what. I am going to be helping out Sam today. Going to houses, checking on people. I'll drop some food off. In fact, I'll check on everyone that has been self-quarantine and see if they need anything."

"Thank you," Michael said.

"Are you okay to do this?" My mother asked.

"I need to do this. Dad is helping."

I said my goodbyes, reiterating to them to stay inside, then my father and I headed down to the Quick Med.

◇◇◇◇

The population of Mills Run, last count, was 1,116 people.

In a matter of days it went from four being sick to thirty the next day. Now Jael had over three hundred people on his list that came to the Quick Med before we returned from Feeny's.

As Sam had said, that wasn't including those who stayed in their homes or even perhaps left to get help.

As chief medical professional and the only medical professional in Mills Run, Sam wanted and needed to gauge where we were as a community.

Although, as sick as my daughter was I couldn't imagine anyone being able to drive to another town to get help.

Still, we needed to know.

My father and I left the house and walked down to Quick Med. We would be two of three workers, until Jael couldn't work anymore.

I believed that until I arrived and saw Brad Rogers at the Quick Med and he wasn't sick. He was there, I suppose to help, I guess. He was carrying a box and handing it to Sam, that surprised me.

I wondered how it benefitted Brad. He never did anything for someone else.

Brad was his own biggest fan. He left Mills Run long before I moved here. A dark blonde haired, blue eyed, pretty boy with a thicker middle. The son of the mayor, Brad was a thirty something, district congressman, self-boasting, rich brat who didn't get the money from his butcher shop mayor father. His maternal grandparents were the condiment queen and king. They gave Brad everything and I swore they bought his election. When he was old enough, he left Mills Run, returning for visits often, just to be annoying. He behaved like he thought because his grandparents were influential and his father was mayor, the town needed to bow down to him.

"Be nice," my father whispered to me when we saw him.

Being nice wasn't on my agenda, I had other things on my mind, dealing with Brad was not one of them. I had just lost my baby girl and he was the last person I wanted to deal with.

We had our differences. When he would ride the ferry he insisted on riding on the bridge as if he were some sort of inspector. The last time I spoke to him, I threatened to throw him overboard.

Sam took the box inside then emerged from Quick Med, he lifted a hand in a wave to me and my father. Brad turned and looked.

He didn't wave.

"I came to help," my father said when he approached Sam. "Whatever you need."

"Thank you. Thank you so much." Sam placed his hands on his hips and looked around. The people no longer lined up at the door, they were further back. Many sat on the ground. "I need to see these folks and get them home, to their beds. I can handle this. I need to know who else is coming. I want to keep the inside of Quick Med pretty clear. Use the tents for those who don't want to leave. There are some cots here, although not many."

"What do you need us to do?" I asked.

"Since you both know the town, I'll put you on that," Sam said. "Brad brought some supplies and can help me out here." Sam walked off toward the people waiting to be seen. He placed a mask over his mouth and approached the first patient.

"Supplies from where?" I asked Brad.

"I grabbed them when I left DC to get my father," Brad replied. "It was bad down there."

"Get you father?" my dad asked. "Where are you taking him? Going into isolation."

"No, there is a place in West Virginia, a friend of mine told me about. A monastery that's taking in people. They have no infection. I was going to take him there and wait it out. Was," Brad corrected. "My father is sick."

"I'm sorry," my father said.

"Me, too. He asked me to help out so that's what I'm doing."

"Well you might wanna put on a mask or something," my father said.

"I don't need one," Brad replied. "I'm immune."

That caught my attention. "How do you know you're immune?"

"I was in DC. Working on the epidemic task force. I was exposed a great deal and they tested me. They almost have a vaccine. Unfortunately, it may be too late."

"What do you mean too late?" my father asked.

"I mean this virus is bad. It's going to run its course and it may take a good bit of the population with it. That's why I wanted to take my father away. Get him secluded until the vaccine was done. There's something else, the virus is ..."

"Where's Jael?" I cut off Brad, it wasn't intentional, it was at that second I noticed Jael wasn't around and I got worried.

"He's inside," Brad pointed to Quick Med.

After saying, "Excuse me," I left the conversation. A half an hour earlier, Jael was out working with people. Him inside worried me, and rightfully so. When I walked in, he was seated on one of the waiting room couches. "Hey," I said softly.

Jael looked horrific. Even worse than a short time earlier.

"Hey," he replied.

"What's going on?"

"I think ... I think I overdid it. I'm not doing well." Jael rubbed his forehead. "I can barely think now. It's getting worse really fast. And I'm ... I'm really cold."

Compassionately, I sighed and sat next to him. "What are you doing? Go home."

He shook his head.

"Listen," I said. "You have the best apartment in Mills Run."

"No."

"It's bright, on the first floor..."

"No."

"You can go to bed, be much more comfortable there."

"No," he repeated.

"Why not?"

Sadly he gazed at me with his glossy eyes. "If I go there, if I leave here, and I die, I'll die alone. At least here if I am on my last breath I just need to look up to see someone. I don't want to see an empty room, Clare. I don't want to be Gordon. I don't want to die alone."

He sounded frightened, which pulled at me and broke my heart.

"That won't happen," I said.

"How can you be sure?"

I reached over and laid my hand on his. "I'll find a way. If ... and I stress if ... if you can't beat this, if this takes you, then I promise you with everything I am, you will not die alone. I won't let it happen."

Jael closed his eyes. He exhaled and after resting his head back, it tilted toward me. He opened then raised his eyes. "Thank you."

I didn't respond verbally. I didn't know what to say. I only nodded and looked at him. My heart broke for him. It was a huge promise I made to him and even though it was going to be so hard to keep, I would do my best to honor it.

I had to. He was my friend and he was sick. No ... he wasn't just sick, Jael, like everyone else who caught the fever ... was dying.

TWENTY-SIX - WINDOW

Helen Jacobs was eighty-two years old on Valentine's Day, she looked much younger and was as spry and energetic as any person half her age. A decade earlier, she had taken over Patsy's Diner when her sister, the owner passed. I wasn't living in town then. I do remember my father telling me the food at the diner was the worst. Helen didn't know what to buy and Patsy had done the cooking. It was an established venue and people still went. It would have gone out of business had it not been for the town reaching out to a cooking network and one of those 'save my restaurant' big time chefs came down and not only was Patsy's back in business, it was better than ever.

At the very least, I expected Helen to be ill.

Armed with a clipboard and two cans of spray paint, I had been given the four streets east of my own street. Basically, we were to go house to house. Knock on the door, shout out that we were checking, if no answer, without forced entry we were to go inside.

I was fine with that.

To Brad's credit, he suggested we use the urban search and rescue markings. Those spray painted markings on a house with a circle, X, and writing. We tweaked it to fit our needs. At the top of the X we would put the date, at the bottom the number of alive, sick or deceased. Our initial went on the left and on the right, we placed an E for empty, Q for self-quarantine, and F for fever.

If we never got into the house or found out, we were not to complete the X. If the house was infected, we used a square around the X instead of a circle. I wrote down the instructions on a Post It, so I wouldn't forget.

It was unnerving.

When I stepped onto Ridge Avenue, it looked so long and desolate. There wasn't a noise or any visible movement.

Helen's house was first. On my lined paper divided into three columns, alive, sick, deceased, I wrote Helen's name and address on the first line.

I knocked, rang the doorbell and then called out. "Helen, it's Clare Ashton, I'm just checking on you for Dr. Sam."

I waited a few seconds and was ready to knock again, when I heard a faint knock. I looked over to the window and Helen stood there, holding back the curtain.

"Are you okay?" I asked. "Are you sick?"

Helen shook her head and her voice was muffled. "I'm fine."

"Good. Good. Stay inside. Do you need anything?"

"No, I'm good. Thank you."

"I'll check on you in a couple days."

Helen gave a thumbs up.

I shook the paint can, marked the house. I gave a Q on the right and at the bottom 1-A, one person alive.

I felt hopeful, maybe a lot of people were like Helen fighting the fever in their own way by staying away, staying inside and staying alive.

TWENTY-SEVEN – SHALLOW

"What are we supposed to do with the bodies?" Sam asked.

We had radios, our means to communicate. Sam put that question out to everyone. Feeny's had announced it wasn't taking anymore dead. They were going to finish up the last of those they had.

"As cold as it sounds," my father said. "We have to rely on the pickup schedule."

"For how long?" Brad asked. "I mean, county will get them only so long before the drivers get sick. There has to be a plan. We need to think. Clare, your thoughts?"

I didn't respond. I had nothing to add. My mind was full. Every door, every report of sickness, I thought of my daughter. I saw her lying on that table at Feeny's. Three times I stopped to sit on the curb and cry.

I was barely done with my first street when my father was starting his third.

I'd check a house, then think of my daughter. Move to another and call my sons. Then Jael occupied my mind. My father had walked him back to his apartment. I wanted to go and see him so I didn't break my promise. I would, after I finished Ridge Avenue.

It was hard. They were people I knew and had seen everyday. It wasn't a news story or something I read online, it was real.

My hope that most people of Mills Run were healthy and in self-quarantine became dashed when I started going door to door.

Some people weren't even home, some had bodies already out for pick up, and some were so sick, I had to enter the home to find them. When I did I marked them down so Sam would come by to give them something. If they lived long enough for him to make his rounds. The fever killed fast. On average it was thirty-six hours. Some though, like Ivy passed away in twenty-four, some lived longer. It reminded me of a quote I heard when learning about the Spanish Flu. *"They were laughing at breakfast, by nightfall we were burying them."*

Too fast. Too scary.

Finding those who would beat the fever seemed impossible. At least on Ridge Avenue. Helen Jacobs was the only person healthy on the street. I didn't know if my father had better luck. I do know he went to check on Sophia and her family, and while they were all healthy, my father wasn't hopeful because Sophia's father had left to get supplies.

He said he'd go back and check on them the next day. Something we both would have to do.

If by some miracle I lived through the fever, I would have to revisit many of the homes to see if those inside beat the fever, or succumbed to it.

Chances were my one visit would be the last. I was convinced the next day would bring the virus to my own front door, or rather front porch, because that was where I'd stay and die as long as my sons and mother were safe inside. I just hoped that one of them, when it was safe, would go to Feeny's to get Ivy. I hated the thought of her never being claimed.

Apparently, and I wouldn't have thought it, Jael had an obsession or maybe fear of what would become of his body when he died.

That didn't cross my mind. To me, I would be dead, what would I know? I didn't have that fear about dying alone. I worried more about those who loved me going through the pain of watching me leave.

Not Jael.

Halfway through my journey on Ridge street I went home, checked on the kids, then headed to Jael's apartment.

My plan was halfway through the street to go visit Jael, then when I was done with the other half to go back. He was part of our radio group, even though he was at home. Yet, I hadn't heard a word from him. It worried me. Especially since Sam told me he believed Jael was sicker longer then he had told us about.

"How do you know? Not second-guessing you as a doctor, but what makes you think that?" I asked.

"Because the nose doesn't start to bleed until the person nears the 24 hour mark."

JAEL's nose had dried blood around it the last I saw him which meant, if he was going to succumb to this virus, he didn't have much time. I wanted to keep true to my promise to be there. So after I had finished spending time with my family for the evening, again, I planned to go back and just stay at his house. It was the least I could do.

There weren't many apartments in Mills Run. There were lots of houses, some trailers, and a new ten unit townhouse development not far out of town. Jael lived in what was the coldest apartment in town. It really was. It was located in the back of Mitzy's flower shop. The outside was graced with a yard which Jael had landscaped beautifully. The apartment was small, but Jael didn't need much. He was barely there. I made my way back into town after my first half of the street was completed and after I visited my sons. To get to Jael's apartment I had to walk around the building and across the beautiful garden. That's when I saw it. Amongst the freshly blooming flower bed was a new hole. It was long, about 3 feet wide, and shallow at two feet deep. If I didn't know any better, it looked like a grave. There was no way. Apparently Jael must've been doing some sort of gardening before he got sick. A new project, he was always starting one.

After knocking to alert my presence, I went inside the quaint apartment. Admittedly, I was a little fearful that something was wrong. Then I heard him cough.

The apartment was only two rooms. A living room kitchen combo and a small bedroom located off of that. I had never been in the bedroom. He kept the door closed when he had company and I was a little shocked when I walked in.

It was very tidy and looked more like something a college student would have. His walls were graced with rock and roll posters, movie themes and sports figures. The blue and brown checkered spread looked like something out of the 1980s. Next to the bed was a dark wooden desk with an attached bookshelf. Not only were there plenty of books, but trophies and ribbons.

Jael was hooked up to it intravenous, little wads of tissue stained with blood were at the foot of his bed. He was even paler if that was possible. His nose had circles of dried blood, his lips were cracked. When he heard me, his eyes opened and he looked up.

"Hey," I said softy. "How are you?"

"I'm okay."

"How's the headache?"

"A little better. The stuff Sam gave me has me kind of floating."

I looked around then grabbed the desk chair, moved it closer to the bed, then sat down. "Nice room."

Jael forced a smile. "This is the way the room looked when I moved in. Everything is the same. I've kept it this way. It has its own charm."

Suddenly I had remembered and I gasped at the fact that I even forgot. Mitzy made that apartment for her son when he was in college. A place where he could be close to her and yet have some sort of independence. Unfortunately, her son had died in an accident long before I even moved to Mills Run, long before Jael rented it. "This was her son's place," I said.

"Yeah," Jael said. "He died before I got to town. I didn't know him. It was decades before she put it up for rent. I was the first person to rent it after he passed. I didn't have the heart to change it. If she couldn't alter it in all those years, then I wouldn't."

I couldn't help but think of how nice that was of him. Then again, he was a really nice guy. That was just Jael's nature. All he ever wanted in life was to belong somewhere and to be loved by someone. That was why he played the field so much, dated so many women. Looking for that special someone. I wished in that moment he had found her.

"So, what's with the hole in the backyard?" I asked. "Are you working on a new project?"

"No," Jael said, "Clare, you know better. You know better, you know what it is."

"How... How did it get there?"

"Brad."

I was flabbergasted. Actually it angered me. "How dare he? How dare you do that?"

"I asked. In fact, he really did offer. I was out there digging it, making my own grave, when he came by to check on me. He took over."

"Jael, why is that important? You don't even know that you're going to die."

"Everybody dies from this," he said. "Everybody."

I lowered my head some and reached out to him even through my gloved hand, I could feel the heat of the skin, it reminded me so much of Ivy at that moment. "I can't stay long. I promise I'll be back tonight to spend the night after the boys are asleep."

"I appreciate it. If it's too much I understand."

"I want to."

I had known Jael for years and knew his every expression. I prided myself that since I spent so much time working with him at the bar I could read his facial expressions and know what he was feeling. In all the years I had known him, I had never seen the one he produced at that moment. Fear.

My friend was scared. He spoke outwardly as if he weren't, but more than his words, his digging a grave and not wanting to be alone, I saw it on his handsome face. "I'll check to see if there's anything you need. Please answer the radio." I gave a squeeze to his arm and as I prepared to leave, I watched him. Jael nodded with closed eyes and pursed his lips.

I lowered my mask and gently kissed him on this forehead. Again, Ivy flashed in my mind, when his skin burned my lips the same way as Ivy's. I knew his temperature was bad and fatally high.

"Why did you do that?" Jael asked. "I'm sick."

"I'm not afraid, not now, not after Ivy. Get some rest. I'll be back."

"Can you put on some music, please. It won't be too quiet. Anything."

"Sure. Where ...."

"By the door."

When I turned to leave, I saw the dresser and on top of it was one of those old boom boxes with a cassette player. I couldn't recall the last time I saw a cassette, let alone stacks of them on top of a dresser. "Yours, or did it come with the room?"

"It came with the room."

There was so much to choose from, everything was at least twenty years old. I saw a Six Pence, None the Richer cassette and after removing the Best of Frank Sinatra cassette, I placed in the new one and pressed play. The moment the music began, Jael closed his eyes. I stared at him for a moment, hoping he'd hold on until I returned and then I walked out to continue my work.

TWENTY-EIGHT – DARK

Mrs. Dawson died, more than likely, not long after her daughter. I stopped in to check on her, and when there was no answer I walked in. I found her sitting in the living room in the wider brown leather reclining chair. Her daughter draped across her lap, Mrs. Dawson's arms dangled down in the position as if, at one time, she was clutching her child. She passed away while holding her. Her little girl was wrapped tightly in a blue knit blanket, probably made by a grandparent or an aunt. Pinned to her chest was a note. It simply read, "My name is Janice Dawson, this is my daughter Lilith. Remember us. "

After swiping my hand down her face to close her eyes, I grabbed a blanket that had been tossed on the couch and covered them both. I would speak to my father as to what we would do. There was supposed to be a pick up, I doubted very much that would happen.

On Ridge Avenue alone, there were bodies. I marked down a dozen . There may have been more. Possibly stacked on one another. It was hard to tell. I wondered what would happen if the trucks never came and no one was there to pick up the bodies. No one was left to bury them. There they would stay, on the side of the road. What about those who survived or possibly even those in the future, when they uncovered the remains of our default civilization? What would they think of what they found? How would they judge us in our final days? Would that be our legacy? That we discarded our dead off to the side, valued no more than our everyday trash. A frail, sick society that went out with a whimper. It was sad.

My mother had made her famous fried chicken. Trying to use the last of the meat that remained in the freezer, that we had not dehydrated. We had two meals left. Anything fresh would have to be frozen in someone else's freezer or we would have to start to rely on our survivor meals. I hated the thought of going into somebody's house and taking their food. We didn't need it. However, should we beat the fever, the items we created to have an extended shelf life, had to be the last things we ate. Consume the perishables first. That was the smart thing to do.

The perishables wouldn't last, though. The electricity went out shortly after we began our meal.

That was when it hit me while I sat on the porch looking into the house lit mainly by the evening sun, my mother preparing the candles, and the windup lanterns. Of all the survivor supplies we got, we never picked up batteries. How did we miss those? They, like other items, were out there. We would just need to get them. With less people in the world, those who lived, those who survived, had so much for the taking. Hopefully it would be used wisely.

Michael paced about frantically. He hadn't charged his phone and feared it was going to die. It took everything I had to convince him he had to stay in the house and Sophia and her family were fine.

No electronics, no television, the last broadcast went out in mid play, so somewhere out there, they had electricity. Just not in Mills Run. If we didn't have it, neither did Steubenville.

I felt bad for my boys and mother, trapped in the house. At least they were safe and healthy. I had an hour long conversation with Eli. We talked about a lot of things, a wide range of topics. It started with talking about Ivy, then moved to other things, always returning to Ivy.

My middle child may had been old enough to know what was going on, but far too young to process such a huge death.

My father had placed plastic over the living room window so we could easily communicate without shouting and our words weren't muffled through double storm windows.

"I wish I played baseball," Eli said.

"You hate baseball," I told him.

"I don't hate watching it. I just didn't like playing because I wasn't any good."

"Then why do you want to play?" I asked.

"Wanted," Eli correct. "I wish I did. Had. What's the correct way?"

"Had. I think." I shrugged.

"Yeah. Because I don't think there's gonna be any baseball teams anymore."

"There will be. One day. Not for a while. So, you'll still get your chance."

Eli glanced over his shoulder to Michael. "He won't ever get another prom."

"No, but who knows. Maybe one day, when things are back to normal, he'll get a chance to do something close to a prom."

"You think it will be normal again?"

At the rate everything was falling apart and from all I had seen I wanted to tell Eli that it wasn't going to happen, there would be a new normal. I didn't know if that was the right thing to do or say to someone his age. Before I could answer my radio crackled.

"Clare, you there?" Jael called out weakly.

I held my finger up to Eli, then lifted the radio. "I'm here."

"When you come back, can you bring batteries for the boom box. It's really quiet."

"I will. I'll be there shortly." I placed down the radio and cringed.

"What's wrong?" Eli asked.

"Forgetting those batteries are already biting me in the ass. Jael needs batteries."

"I was gonna say Ivy has batteries in those robot things she has." Eli lowered his head. "But I don't want to give away anything of Ivy's. Not yet. Not ever. Even batteries."

"Neither do I," I said staring at Eli. I just wanted to hold him. I knew that's what he needed. I couldn't, he needed to be away from me.. My mother's arms would have to be the substitute.

There was a noise behind me, I knew it had to be my father. I turned around and saw him walking up the path.

"You've been out a while," I said.

"I just wanted make some distance." He set a spray paint can on the porch. "Are you heading down to see Jael?"

"I was going to in a little bit."

"I think you should go sooner than later. I was just there. He's not doing well. I left a lantern for him."

""He asked me to bring batteries for his boom box."

"I saw that. Those take the big batteries."

"I'll stop at the drug store. Sam got the door open." I stood and then looked at Eli. "I'm going to go see Jael. You're feeling okay, right?"

"Yeah, I'm good. I'll talk to Pap." He placed his hand on the plastic. "Night, Mom."

I pressed my hand against his. "Night, Sweetie, I love you."

"I love you, too."

I shouted to Michael. "Good night, Michael."

Michael looked at me and nodded.

My father handed me the hand held spotlight. "I'll talk to Michael."

"Thank you." I squeezed his hand when I walked by him and before I left our property I glanced back once more to Eli who remained at the window.

The sun had long since set and night was upon Mills Run. Without a full moon, street lights, or illumination from homes, it was really dark. My eyes adjusted half way into town and a Sixpence None the Richer remake of *'Don't Dream It's Over'* was stuck in my head. A remake by them that seemed to be a perfect mental orchestration backdrop for the quiet eeriness about everything.

I stopped at the drug store, stumbled my way through until I found the batteries I needed. Oddly things weren't disturbed. No looting, no rushing for last minute supplies. Mills Run was headed quietly into its downfall.

As I left the drug store, I noticed the orange glow of candles coming from The Pepper Mill. It carried out to the side walk. Curious, I crossed the street just before Mitzy's and looked inside. The door was open and Sam sat at the bar with two kerosene lanterns.

I flicked off my spotlight, leaned against the door and cleared my throat. "What's going on?"

"Taking a break. I always came here at the end of my day." Sam lifted a bottle. "Jael ..." He paused. "He let me in."

I nodded and sniffed, then walked in. "Are you okay?"

"Oh, Clare, I'm tired, I'm sad ... I can't even grieve my own father's death because I'm not alone in this. You know?" he looked at me. "Yes, you do know."

"I do." I walked over to the bar, lifted a shot glass and poured a half shot of bourbon, downing it immediately. "How are things are Quick Med?"

"Quiet." Sam swished the liquor around in his glass then sipped. "And ... it will be a lot more quiet in the morning." He took another drink. "It sucks. Right now, Brad is on watch."

I huffed out a breath.

"He's trying."

"You can't make up years of being a dick in a single afternoon."

"He's immune. He's trying to get all his human contact in now. He'll be the last one standing."

"How unfair is that?" I shook my head. "I was taught to live a good life and I'd be rewarded somehow. He lives a selfish life and he lives."

"How is that a reward?" Sam asked. "To be one of the few in this god forsaken wasteland of a world," he said it almost bitterly, pouring a bit more in his glass.

"If you need me. I'm around. I'm heading to Jael's now."

Sam sighed out so heavily I heard it. "In a strange way the three of us were friends. Closing this bar down every night. You working, me sitting here and Jael sitting at the end of the bar trying to find a date on line before he had his one and only tequila."

That made me laugh. A small one. "He always tried. And yes," I said, leaning into him as I walked by. "We are friends. I'm going to say goodbye to my friend right now."

Sam's head lowered. "Tell him I ..." He pointed to a glass at the end of the bar. "I poured him a drink. I wish he was here to drink it."

I looked at glass at the end of the bar, it had alcohol in it and a bottle was next to it.

"How about ..." I walked over and grabbed the bottle, then three glasses. "We take the party to him? Come with me, Sam. He doesn't want to be alone. We always ended the night with the three of us. How about the three of us end ..." I cringed and closed my eyes. "How about it?"

Sam downed his drink and grabbed his bottle of Jack. "Yeah, I'd like that."

I waited for him and we walked out together. We only needed to cross the street and go a half a block.

I radioed Jael to let him know we'd be there in a few minutes. Begging in my mind that he'd answer. I was relieved when he did. He sounded weak.

When we got there his apartment wasn't completely dark. My father left him a lantern and three bottles of water that were untouched. Sam had replenished his IV earlier and there was still some left.

Jael pulled himself to a sitting position when we walked in. His glossy eyes filled with a bit of life when he saw us. I propped pillows behind him to make him comfortable. I would be lying if I said I wasn't hoping he was one in the million that would beat it. After all, he seemed so strong at that point even with the Fever, others were unconscious.

Sam immediately poured him a drink, while I fumbled to replace the batteries in the old cassette player.

"It burns my mouth," Jael said. "I don't care."

After I finished putting the batteries in I pressed the power button. I was unsure if batteries would even work in such an old player. "Hey, it works." I noticed the cassettes weren't neat and stacked, but scattered. "Who was going through these?" I asked and looked back at Jael.

"Everyone." He held his glass to Sam. "Keep them coming please."

I ejected the cassette in the player. "Oh, man, who was playing you Menudo?"

"That would be me," Sam said. "I thought since Jael is Latino, he might enjoy a Latino boy band."

"That's not funny," I said.

"Yes it is," Jael replied. "It was better than Brad's choice. He played country. Your dad he played ..."

I lifted the tape. "Sex Pistols."

"Yes, I like what you played the best."

"Then that's what we'll listen to." I sought out the Sixpence None the Richer cassette and put it in and prepared to press play.

"Can we ..." Sam spoke up. "Not. Not yet. Just sit here the three of us, Clare? Now would be a good time."

There was something about the tone of Sam's voice that he was trying to convey urgency to me. I nodded that the cassette could wait, turned around to see Sam helping Jael drink from the glass.

I walked over and sat on Jael's bed while Sam sat in a chair.

"How are you?" Jael asked me. His breaths were shallow, his voice soft.

"Me? I'm good. Sad, but good. The boys are healthy at least."

Jael nodded. "I'm glad you two are here."

"Have another sip buddy," Sam said, holding the glass to Jael's mouth. "One more. Okay?"

Jael took a sip, the liquid ran down the corner of his mouth. Sam wiped it.

I made eye contact with Sam and he shook his head.

"Another night together. The three of us," Jael said. "Thank you. Thank you guys."

"It's my pleasure," I said.

Jael closed his eyes for a second and took a breath. "It's not bad now. Not at all."

"Really?" I asked. "Tell me about it. I need to know what my daughter went through."

"At the end, I don't think she suffered Clare," he spoke with labored breaths. "She didn't. At first, the headache is bad and your body burns so bad you want to scream. There's no energy. None. Then ..." He dropped his hand on mine. "It's starts to be okay. I don't feel bad right now. I feel okay." He looked at Sam then back to me. His eyes locked on to mine. "I'm surprised. I feel good."

"It's the tequila," Sam said.

"Maybe." Jael smiled at me. "Right now, I feel like I will beat this."

"Good. You fight." I told him. "Fight."

His little finger rolled under my hand. "I am, Clare. I ..."

It was as if Jael was put on pause. He didn't move, he didn't blink, he's eyes just stared out blankly.

Immediately the room was overcome with a hushed peacefulness.

I gasped and lost my breath. "Sam?" I peeped out his name.

Sam reached up and felt for a pulse. "He's gone."

"How? How?" I whimpered. "He was just talking. He was just fine."

"No, he wasn't. He wasn't fine. He was just waiting on someone to be here."

Instantly I felt his warm hand cool down and I lowered my head.

He was gone. My friend was gone. That fast. I didn't get to say goodbye or tell him how much I appreciated him in my life. I felt like an idiot, unable to move or think.

Sam reached up and closed Jael's eyes and then he stood and walked away.

I didn't see what he was doing, I couldn't take my eyes of Jael. Waiting for him to move, to breathe, he never did.

I heard the 'click' of the cassette player.

"He's said he liked your choice," Sam said. "So, it's for Jael." He returned, sat down and lifted his glass as the music began. "To Jael, my friend." He finished his drink.

We sat quietly without saying a word, a silent homage to our friend as *Don't Dream it's Over* played.

I made a promise to Jael, one I kept. He didn't want to leave this world alone … and he didn't.

TWENTY-NINE - DRIVER'S SEAT

April 25

I felt it. There was another hole in my heart and it just added to the pain. It took me a moment to determine what it was. Heartache wasn't just an emotion it was a physical ailment that flared up causing intense pain with each breath, each memory.

It started with Ivy.

It grew with Jael.

Would my heart be able to sustain anymore?

I radioed my father that we were staying until sunup. I could have gone home, but everyone was sleeping and Sam just didn't want to leave Jael's room.

Sam sat in that chair, hands folded, elbows on his thighs staring at Jael. He was a doctor and he was lost for answers.

We stayed there, not saying a word, music playing in the background, as if waiting for Jael to wake up. He only turned darker, colder and stiff.

He was gone.

Just as the sky began to lighten, we carried Jael outside and placed him in the grave he had already dug. I felt envious, he was buried at home. I truly wish I would have done that with Ivy. Created a grave, one I could visit. I thought about bringing her ashes to Jael's garden. It was so beautiful and the perfect resting place. Perhaps create a spot next to Jael.

"I'll make a marker for this," Sam said. "It's needs a marker."

I nodded and took the shovel from his hands. "Get some rest."

"What for?" He inhaled. "I mean, I'm going to head to Quick Med and no one will be breathing."

"You don't know that," I said.

"Okay, I don't. There will be a few on their last breath, then another round will start."

"Sam ..."

"I hate this, Clare. I hate this virus."

"Me, too." I rested the shovel against the fence and my head lifted up when I heard the air brakes. "County is making rounds."

"That surprises me."

"Maybe it's just our town, maybe the rest of the world isn't completely down and out," I suggested.

Sam laughed an airy, 'doubtful' and shook his head.

"Let's go," I said. "I have to get home."

"Go on. I'm going to stay here."

"I'll check on you. Are you feeling okay?"

"Me? Unfortunately, I'm fine."

I didn't know how to respond, I just knew I didn't like the way he said that. It was an odd reply. I walked out of the backyard, around the building to the street and I saw the truck. I thought about asking the driver how things were out there. However, I wasn't getting any answers. The driver was Brad.

He stood by the open driver's door. "I'm sorry about Jael."

"Thanks. What's ... what's going on? Why do you have that?"

"I took a ride about an hour ago to Steubenville and ... the trucks were just sitting there. It's quiet there. Nobody on the streets. Just quiet. No one was coming. So, I brought it here. Figured we could maybe start getting the ..."

"And do what?" I cut him off. "Load them in the truck, then what?"

"Three miles downriver is the old Thompson Steele barge. It's sitting there empty."

"You wanna take our neighbors, the people of this town, put them in a dump truck them toss them on a barge?"

"I'm trying to help here, Clare. I promised my father or I would have been gone," Brad snapped. "I'm not going to be here for long. I plan on hitting that monastery, there's life there. You can't stay here with all these bodies. As cold as that sounds, they are no longer alive. It'll be a mess around here in a week."

"Well, good thing for me I won't be around." I turned and started to walk.

"You really think that?" Brad shouted. "You're still here. You aren't sick."

"Not yet. It's just a matter of time," I said as I walked. "I will be dead."

"What if you don't get sick and die?"

I didn't answer, I just kept on walking. The thought of not dying hadn't even crossed my mind. I didn't want to think that far ahead. My focus was on the here and now, at that moment it was more so on getting home.

Halfway up my street my legs felt like rubber, total body and mental exhaustion hit me. I knew that once I got to my house, I would pass out on the porch. I was run down or I was sick. For the most part I had resolved myself to having the virus by the end of the day. There was no way I wouldn't.

When I arrived at my house, I was only thinking about getting rest. I was pretty snippy with Brad, and even though he annoyed me, it wasn't fair to him. After I rested I would apologize. There things I needed him to do, especially since he wouldn't be around after it was all said and done. One of them was to go to Feeny's and get Ivy's ashes if I couldn't.

I walked across my driveway focused on the house and my father's SUV was sitting there. I didn't think anything of it until I saw my father in the driver's seat.

He held onto the wheel, staring forward.

It was odd so I walked over tapping the window. "Dad?" I called out. "Where are you going?"

Slowly, he turned and looked at me. The moment he did, I saw it on his face and his eyes, a sickening feeling hit my gut.

My father had it.

"No." I said.

He lowered the window only a smidgeon. "It came for me, Clare."

"No." I shook my head.

"I think I should stay in here. It's safer that way."

I shook my head. "You are not staying in this truck. You hear me? I'll take you to the house, the ferry, or anyone of those two, but you are not going to go through this sitting in your truck alone."

"I'm alright. I don't want to get near you, your mother or the boys. All that matters is you are all healthy and fine."

"Daddy." My hand laid flush on the window. In the early morning hours and intense quiet, sound magnified. I heard the squeak of the screen door and the sound of footsteps on the wooden porch.

"Clare," my mother called my name.

My mother walked from the house? I stepped away from the SUV and looked. "Mom? Get back inside. I need to figure out …"

"Clare," she said stronger, folded her arms tight to her body then whimpered my name. "Clare."

I walked toward the porch. "Are you sick?"

She shook her head.

I exhaled in relief.

"But Eli is," she said.

Her words were another punch to my gut. I shook my head. "Are you sure?"

Again, she whimpered and nodded.

I felt my entire body tense up and I just wanted to scream out. My hands clenched and I went from looking at the SUV to the house.

Somehow, someway it had to all be a bad dream.

Oh my God this wasn't happening.

First my daughter, my precious baby girl. Then my friend, now my father and my son? Even if the world wasn't going to end, at that moment in time, I knew my world was slipping from my grip and there was nothing I could do to stop it.

<><><><>

There was no way my father was going to suffer the fever in the front seat of his SUV, and there was no way my son was going to suffer through it without his mother's touch, love and comfort. The moment I raced into the house and my hand touched upon Eli's fevered skin, I did something not even I expected I would do. I panicked and freaked out.

Completely out of character for me, I spun on my heels and in a state of utter confusion and fear, I bolted from the house. My heart beat out of control with every pounding step on the pavement I wheezed out my heartache. It had to be a nightmare, it couldn't be true.

No. No. No.

I kept running, I couldn't stop. As if I kept on running, I could get so far away it would no longer be true.

But it was.

I ran nearly five blocks without getting winded. I just couldn't stop. Where was I going? What did I plan on doing? I stopped just as I hit the edge of Quick Med parking lot.

There my breathing caught up to me and I fought to inhale. It was a struggle. My shoulders heaved up and down as I stepped slowly and cautiously into the parking area.

It was full of people camping out, they were on sleeping bags, cots, or sitting against each other to stay up. They were people we knew, our neighbors and friends…

And they weren't moving.

There had to be hundreds. Carefully, I walked around them. Each face I saw caused a whimper to escape me.

Allyson Cramer

Jennifer Higgins

Mr. and Mrs. Higgins.

Too many names, too many faces.

"Bill." He worked for my father and there he was slumped on a rolled up sleeping bag. I nudged him with my foot. His eyes were closed, maybe he was sleeping. "Bill, get up. Bill … Bill, wake up."

Nothing.

No one was making a noise. Not a cough, moan or whimper.

Sam was right.

He said no one would be breathing and nobody was.

If ever there was a punch of reality it was right then and there. Three good breaths and I grunted out loudly, turning left to right, back and forth, looking around until I grew dizzy.

Then the silence was broken and the voices began. They meshed together, over lapping, one after another.

"Help me."

"Don't let me die."

"I'm so sick."

"Clare, Clare…. Don' let them take me."

I covered my ears, the voices were still there. Louder, ever so loud.

I tried to move, to turn and get out of there. I was trapped by everything in my path. The bodies around me were like quick sand, keeping me immobile. Hands reached for me, grabbing my legs, ankles.

"God!" I cried out and then from the depths of my soul I let out this ungodly scream. I didn't even know I had it in me. It was loud, long and deep. I couldn't stop screaming.

"Clare!" Sam called out my name abruptly, as he held my arms and jolted me once.

I stopped.

The silence returned.

There was no one calling for help, no one reaching for me.

"Clare." He stared at me. "Stop."

My head lowered and I started to cry. I wanted to tell him my father was sick, Eli was but I didn't. Not right then, because I couldn't stop crying.

THIRTY - FLIGHT

My breakdown was something that needed to happen. At least, that was what Sam said. I took a few more minutes at Quick Med, got myself together, then Sam and I headed to my house.

For my father and Eli, I had to be strong. Hating to acknowledge it, I knew I was going to lose them and I wasn't going to spend what time I had left with them focusing on my pain.

The task of moving bodies was daunting for Brad, I could see that. I doubt any of us were going to be able to do it. There were so many bodies in the parking lot, not to mention the ones on the street, in other houses.

When we arrived at my house, Sam did what he could for Eli, hooking him up to an IV, keeping him comfortable.

Eli groaned out, "It hurts. It hurts, Mom. Please. It hurts."

I begged Sam to give Eli as much as he could do so he would be comfortable. I remembered what Jael had told me about how painful it was. While I wanted my son to be awake, to talk to me, I didn't want him to suffer. Eventually the medication would wear off, and like Jael, hopefully, I'd get those moments with him.

I wasn't going to make the same mistake with him that I did with Ivy. I worried so much about getting help, her last hours were away from the things she knew; home, family and her bed.

Eli was still awake when Michael came into the room. He wore a mask and gloves as he stood in the doorway staring.

"Mom, can I ... can I talk to Eli?" he asked.

"Sure. Please keep a distance."

Michael nodded.

Eli was still conscious and awake, he wouldn't be for long. I kissed his forehead. "Mike wants to talk to you. Okay?"

"Michael," Eli whimpered.

"Hey, Buddy." Michael walked in.

I moved out of the way. I wanted to check on my father. I paused in the doorframe when I heard Michael talking to Eli.

"You scared, Eli?"

"I'm too sick."

"I know."

"Are you?" Eli asked.

"Heck, yeah. I know you're gonna beat this."

"Ivy didn't."

A lump formed in my throat and I felt it travel to my stomach. I folded my arms tighter to my body and turned. Michael was reassuring Eli and I was going to give them their time.

I walked from the room expecting my father to be in his room, he wasn't.

My father was his own entity and insisted he wanted to be on the back porch. My mother was in the kitchen hanging a piece of plastic over the window so she could talk to him. He was outside, feet propped up on the ottoman, an IV pole at his side and a blanket draped across his lap.

"I don't know if I can stay away from Eli," my mother said. "It seems so cruel to stay away because he's sick. Your father ... that's a different thing?" she sniffled. "My heart is broken, Clare, I don't know how you're handling it so well."

"I'm not. I'm really not." I opened the back door and stepped on the porch. "You know we have a perfectly fine bedroom, Dad."

"I don't want to be like everyone else," my father said. "Dying in a bed. No one finds you. I just want to be original."

"You don't know that you're going to die."

"Clarabelle." He shook his head. "We know the truth."

"There are people that have beaten it," I told him as I crouched down by him. "There are."

"No one in town has."

"Well, then that increases your odds."

"I'd rather give those odds to Eli."

"Would you be mad at me if I said, me, too?"

He chuckled. "I'd expect no less."

"I love you."

"I love you, too."

As I leaned forward to kiss him, the back door opened and Michael stepped.

"I can't do this," Michael said. "I can't. I have to do something. I have to help, I have to …"

"No!" I said hard. "You will stay secluded until this thing is done."

"It's already in the house, Mom, what difference does it make?" Michael asked. "Let me get out there and do something. Let me go door to door and check on people."

"No."

"Then at least let me go check on Sophia."

"No," I was adamant.

"I've been in this house two weeks."

"You'll stay two more if that's what it takes to keep you alive."

"There's more to living than just staying alive."

"Don't." I stood up and faced him. "You can't throw that at me. You're arguing with the wrong person on that. I watched one child leave this earth and now I am losing another. I'll pick staying alive for you right now, thank you very much. You are my child."

"And …" My father spoke up. "You are mine, Clare. I can't make that choice for you. You can't make that choice for Michael."

"He's a child."

"He's not five. He's not ten. He's an intelligent young man, Clare…" My father looked up at me. "I wish I could lock you in a room, but what are you doing? You don't even have a mask on. You locked Eli in this house and he still got sick. Let Michael do what he needs to do. Let him at least go see his girlfriend."

I exhaled and looked from my father to my son.

"Please, Mom."

"Promise me you won't go into their house. For their sake and yours. Promise me."

"I promise. Thank you. I'll keep the mask on, too." He pointed to it and then, mask over his lips he darted a kiss to my cheek. "Thank you. Thank you, Pap." Without hesitation, he took off.

My father's hand was in the air in a wave.

His leaving didn't feel right to me. A part of me was hurt that he didn't want to stay. "Is his girlfriend more important than you or Eli? I'm so confused."

"Eh, I don't think that's the case," he said. "Leaving, going over there, it's not more important. It's just easier than seeing what's happening here. Understand?"

I did. The truth was in the house, or on the streets of Mills Run, it was all the same. None of it was easy.

<><><><>

There were two single beds in Eli's room. One was his, the other's was Michael's. It didn't take much to convince my father to take Michael's bed. I explained to him that I didn't want to choose who, or when, I took care of each of them. Eli would also be less afraid if my father was right next to him.

It was hard for my father to lose Ivy and it was breaking his heart to watch Eli. Maybe that was why he was so reluctant to be right next to him.

My mother stayed in the room, as well. We didn't need conversation from my father or Eli, we just needed time with them.

My mother looked worn and drawn, I kept asking her if she felt alright. She said she wasn't sick, she was just heart broken. I understood that. I kept asking myself why. What I had done so horribly in my life that warranted such a punishment as watching my children leave this earth? I hadn't even had time to grieve Ivy and now I watched Eli. His fever spiked and stayed high, he didn't respond and his breathing was shallow.

I had to remember it wasn't a punishment. As much as it hurt, as much as I hated it, I would rather be the one to go last rather than first. I was there to take care of them. Who would be there if I wasn't?

I wasn't unique to the heartache of losing children to the virus. The woman I met on the way to Steubenville was a reminder of that fact. I wasn't alone, or even one of a hundred. I was one of billions of mothers holding their child, praying for a miracle that they knew would probably never come.

A few hours into the afternoon, after not leaving the room, I heard the front door open and I figured it was Michael, or Sam. Until I heard the call of my name.

It was Brad.

I told my mother I would be right back and went downstairs to find him standing in my living room. "What's wrong?" was my greeting, because to me, the only reason he would be standing there was if something was wrong.

Brad shook his head. "Nothing. I'm ... I'm sorry for what's happening to your family."

"Thank you."

"I brought you a small generator. It's on the front porch. I want you to charge your phone. I don't know how much longer we'll have service, I'm guessing not much longer, but I want to be able to reach you."

"Why?"

"I'm going to head to Wayne tomorrow morning and look for that sanctuary monastery."

"Why tomorrow?"

"Why not? I need a break from this. I need to see something positive."

"Is it real?" I asked. "Is it a virus free zone?"

"I don't know. I only know what I was told. I need to check it out. It can be some sort of holy ground thing. I don't know. I can wait until …"

"No." I cut him off. "Go."

"I'll be back soon."

"It doesn't matter."

"Yeah, it does. Everything is falling apart Clare. There will be so few of us left. We have to stick together."

"Go to the monastery. If there are people there, that's where you need to be. I'm not going to beat this thing."

"You really believe that?" Brad asked. "You really believe you're going to get sick."

"I do."

"If you don't have it and Sam doesn't, then maybe you are immune."

"No, I'm just a mom and I have mother immunity."

He tilted his head in confusion.

"Two years ago everyone came down with this horrible stomach flu. It was bad. Everyone was sick but me. When everybody was fine, then I got sick. It wasn't the first time. It was always that way. I never got sick because I had to take care of everyone, then after I did, it hit me. This is no different. It's the mother immunity factor. It's short lived, just like this will be."

"You don't know. I'm immune. So immunity is real."

That's when it hit me. Brad said he was tested. He was immune, which meant he was safe. Even if the place in West Virginia was a myth, Brad was safe to be around.

"You said this place is in the mountains?" I asked.

"Yeah."

"Will you be going through any towns?"

"Not unless I have to. Why?"

I nodded. "Will you take Michael to this sanctuary?"

"Is that what you want?"

"Yes, I want my child safe. You're immune. He's not sick. Will you take him away from Mills Run? I'll charge my phone, you can stay in touch."

"Of ... of course."

"Thank you. Will you find him? He's been gone for a few hours and I can't leave."

"He's not here?"

"No. He's probably sitting in front of his girlfriend's house on Bank. They are self-quarantining."

"I'll go over and check on him."

"Thank you. It's the very last house on the left."

Brad turned to walk out and stopped. "Oh, Clare. Please. Charge your phone."

I held up a finger, went into the kitchen, grabbed my phone and returned, handing it to Brad. "Here."

"I'll charge it. I'll go tell him and I'll be right back."

After thanking him, I headed back up to Eli's room. I didn't want to send my son away, I didn't want to send him with Brad, yet if there was a chance to keep him alive and healthy, then I was going to take that chance.

I told my mother about my plan. I guess I needed her approval or something.

My father chimed in. As sick as he was, he was still talking. "You don't even know Brad is really immune," my father said.

"He was tested," I replied. "He hasn't worn a mask or gloves and he's not sick. Besides, he's too much of a dick to not be one of the ones who remain."

"Can't be that much of a dick if he's helping so much," my father said.

My father didn't have much to say on whether me sending Michael away was a good idea. My mother on the other hand was more insightful.

"What if he doesn't want to go?" she asked. "Then what?"

I started to believe that was the case. That Michael told Brad to 'get lost' and Brad continued on his self-appointed task of, 'Body Clean Up Man'.

I thought that as the hours passed, then I started to get worried when it grew dark.

Then it dawned on me that my phone was charging. I could call Brad or Michael to find out what was going on. If that wasn't successful, hating to do so, I'd get in the car and head to Sophia's house myself.

Michael had been gone far too long without checking in.

The second I got to my living room the front door opened and Brad walked in. He looked distraught and panicked.

"What is it? What's wrong?" I asked. "I haven't heard from you in hours."

"I didn't want to not have answers."

"What? What are you talking about?"

His hand shook as he extended a piece of paper. "I went to Bank Street. Last house on the left. I found this."

Apprehensively I took the paper from his hand. It had a piece of tape on it and it was folded.

"It was on the door," Brad said.

I turned my back to Brad as I opened it.

It read: 'Sophia and her family are sick. They need help. I took them to find help. Michael."

I wheezed out.

"I looked," Brad said. "I got in my truck and I drove around hoping to catch them. I didn't have a direction. I'm sorry."

I was sick. Sick, angry and devastated. My son had left without saying goodbye. He left Mills Run. He was out there somewhere. The question was where?

THIRTY-ONE – DIRECT LINE

April 26

More than anything I wanted to focus on Michael, but I couldn't Although I tried calling him over and over, even sending him texts that it was okay what he did, I just needed to know that he was alright. Each attempt was met with silence.

He was not responding.

Brad volunteered to go check out med camps. I had been to one, I knew they were nearly impossible to navigate. He insisted he try. Thinking like a teenager I tried to figure out where Michael would go for help. It wouldn't be Steubenville, he knew that was futile after what happened to Ivy.

My oldest son was out there somewhere and I didn't know what I was going to do. I wanted to think about it, find a solution, focus on Michael, but Eli was the center of my attention. He had to be. His small hands curled tightly around my fingers as he struggled to breathe.

I was too focused on Eli's fingers gripping tightly to mine as he fought for each and every breath. Eli knew I was there, he needed me. He deserved for me to give him my all, which I did.

Eli was an innocent boy who believed in the magic of video games and didn't doubt Santa until after he was ten.

I watched my son, held his hand, told him stories and conveyed my love.

I did everything I could. He never got less than a hundred percent of my attention. Even when my phone made a noise, I only shifted my eyes away from Eli to see if it was Michael.

It never was and I returned to watching Eli. My chair next to him, my face near his.

I was hopeful because both he and my father made it well into the next morning. Beyond the twenty-four hour mark.

Then Eli's breathing became labored. Each breath was pronounced. I could feel the air he expired hit against my nose. I wanted them all. I wanted to feel each and every breath.

I focused on them, listening to the sound, the rhythm.

In, out.

In, out.

In … out.

In.

At one minute after eleven in the morning, my youngest son took his last breath.

I wallowed in heartbreak and sadness. I gripped his head, bringing it close to mine and silently sobbed. I couldn't speak, I couldn't tell my mother that he was gone. Not yet. Then as I took in those first few seconds of the loss of my child, my mother softly called out.

"Daddy's gone."

Clutching Eli, I groaned out and then I wept. My father and my son left this earth at the same time. I wanted so much to believe in an afterlife at that moment, to believe that somehow they were together looking down and saying, "We're okay."

I was consumed with pain.

Too much pain.

The entire situation was incomprehensible and unbearable.

How would I even manage to pry myself away from that room, away from my father and Eli?

I realized I had to and didn't have a choice, I lifted my eyes to look at my mother.

She was seated between the two beds, holding my father's hand. Her face mask was off, as were her gloves.

My mother's dark eyes and pale face said more than any words could of.

There was no denying the fact that my mother was ill. Like everyone else, she had the fever.

<><><><>

I hated to do so, I really did. It felt rushed and disrespectful, but everything was falling apart so fast I couldn't keep up.

I covered my son and father, closed the door and promised to make my goodbyes right by them after I helped my mother.

Taking her downstairs, I placed her on the sofa. She kept flinging out her hand and saying she was fine.

"What hurts?" I asked. "What's bothering you?"

"I'm fine."

"Head, fever …?"

"I'm fine."

I covered her. "I'm going to go get Sam. The IV will help against the fever."

"Clare, there is no help with this." She grabbed my arm.

"Let me go get Sam."

"Sweetheart," she said softly. "I don't think that's going to help. I don't think … we should look for Sam to help."

I started to dismiss her words. After all Sam was always there. He always helped. He was always around.

The moment I thought that, it hit me. I hadn't seen Sam since the morning before. I hadn't seen or heard from him for a long time.

Twenty-four hours.

That wasn't typical of Sam.

Instantly, I grew worried and then I remembered my phone. I had gotten several messages. None were from Michael, that was the only name I looked for. I couldn't recall if Sam reached out. Surely he had.

I found my phone and looked.

Four messages.

All from Brad.

'Just woke up. Have a few more bodies then heading out to Wheeling and Washington Pa. Aid Stations there.'

'Finished. Heading out. Will keep you posted."

"Please check on Sam. Just looked in. He's not well."

"Have you heard from Sam or Michael?"

"Oh my God," I whispered.

"What is it?" my mother asked.

I shook my head, replied to Brad that things were bad and I just saw his messages. I would get back to him.

"I'll be right back," I told my mother.

"What's wrong?"

"Nothing. I want to get medication from Quick Med."

"There's no need," my mother said.

I paused before the door. "I want to go check on Sam."

That was all I told her. I didn't mention Brad's messages about Sam because I didn't believe it. Sam had held off, like me, this entire time. He was tired, that was all. No way, no how, was Sam sick.

She nodded her understanding and I headed out.

I tried not to look around as I walked, tried not to see the stillness and quiet of my home town.

When I got close to Quick Med, I could see how hard at work Brad had been.

The parking lot full of bodies was cleared. Those who had been there and died were placed in one of four large mounds. At first I thought he had moved them all by hand, then I noticed the county snow removal truck. He had moved them aside as best as he could. I wasn't going to judge that.

Since we had no bodies bags I could see blue tarps that flapped with each breeze, covering the bodies. He probably got those from the country office as well, because they were the same tarps that were used to cover the road salt piles in storage.

Despite the bodies being covered, I could catch the odor in the air. It was still soon after they died, it would only get worse.

There was such a quiet to Mills Run you could hear any little sound. Noise traveled. I caught the sound of music as I neared the door and when I reached for it, I knew it came from inside.

I opened the door, the music was slightly louder, and I recognized it right away. It was Sixpence Non the Richer. Did Sam take that old player and tape from Jael's apartment?

The song finished the second I stepped into the lobby and then there was silence.

"Sam?" I called out.

No response.

The clinic was empty, I expected people inside, there weren't any. I walked slowly down the corridor toward Sam's office, peeking in every exam room.

Sam's door was slightly ajar, I knocked once, calling out, "Sam." I pushed the door open.

The back of his chair was too me, a gallon bottle of Jack Daniels was on his desk.

Frightened, I called out once more, "Sam. Sam, please don't be dead."

The chair turned slowly.

I exhaled in relief until I saw him.

"Not yet. Soon," Sam said, lifting a glass from his desk and downing the liquid.

"Oh, Sam." I said softly. It was apparent he was sick, very sick. "I'm so sorry I didn't call you or check on you."

"You had your own things to worry about. I'm sorry I didn't answer you when you called my name. I was concentrating on getting the shunt in," he said. "Difficult when you're drunk. I'm a little drunk. I just haven't attached the bag." He lifted a plastic IV bag and put in on his desk.

The fluid inside the bag was tan.

"What is that?" I asked.

"Jack."

"Sam."

"I'm going to feed it straight in. I told you that was how I was going out."

"Sam, you'll die in minutes."

"I will." Sam refreshed his glass and downed it. "Better fast than slow. It's how I want to go out."

"What if you aren't meant to die from this?"

Sam smiled. "You know, you say that to everyone."

"One of these times I'll be right."

"Not this time." He poured more. "How's your dad? Eli?"

I shook my head. "My mother is sick now."

"I'm sorry."

"Me, too."

"Michael?"

I huffed out a breath. "He left. He said he was visiting Sophia and took them somewhere for help. I don't know where. I can't get in touch with him. Brad is out looking now."

"You'll find him. He's young and how far can he go? You'll find him."

"What can I do for you, Sam?"

"Say Goodbye. I'm going to finish this…" he lifted the glass. "Then hook up the bag, sit back, reconcile some things and take my last breath."

"I can stay."

"No, I'm not Jael," he smiled. "This is my private moment. I'd rather we say goodbye when I can look at you."

"Very well. Please know, it has been a pleasure knowing you and being your friend."

"Ditto." He lifted his glass. "You brightened my Saturdays here."

"Thank you. I'll leave you be." I took a step back. "Sam?"

"Yeah."

"I'm sure gonna miss you."

"Thank you."

I turned to walk out.

"Clare?" He called my name. "There is something you can do for me."

"What's that?"

With his hand holding the glass, he pointed. "The cassette should be done rewinding. Can you press play, and pull the door closed when you leave?"

"Absolutely." I reached to the player, it was Jael's and I pressed play. "Goodbye, Sam."

"Goodbye, Clare."

I walked from the office and closed the door.

The music started playing, it brought back the feeling of Jael's room. Maybe Sam liked that peacefulness, I didn't know. I stayed there for a moment, listening, thinking of Sam and his final moments, and then as he requested, I gave him his privacy and I moved on.

On the way home, I hummed the last song I heard on that tape player, my way of sharing it mentally with Sam. I felt as if I were the world's saddest woman on earth. With the way people were dying, I probably was.

I started to really worry. I hadn't heard from Brad since he sent those text messages hours earlier. He didn't even respond to the two I recently sent him.

And Michael ...

It had been twenty-four hours since I had seen or heard from my son.

I had to figure out what I was going to do. If Brad didn't find him, where would I go? Did he even make it to a medical camp, or was he stuck on a road somewhere?

I returned home with no medication for my mother. I felt horrible. Although, from what I had seen, I didn't think the medication made all that much of a difference really. Maybe some wine or vodka would have the same numbing effect.

She was laying on the couch when I walked in.

"No luck at Med Quick?" she asked.

"I'm sorry."

"It's fine. I gave birth to you without anything. I can't see dying of a flu being much worse. The end result is close to the same. A different joy and relief. Plus, I took some ibuprofen."

I wanted to tell her the fever was a heck of a lot bigger than over the counter painkillers, but I didn't. She had ice on her head and lounged back.

I sat on the coffee table. "Sam's sick."

"Oh, no. How is he?"

"Drunk."

"That's not a bad thing."

"He's got an IV set up to pour booze right into his veins. He's taking the fast route out."

"That's not a bad idea either."

I reached out and rested my hand on her arm. "Oh, wow, you're so fevered."

"I know." She took a deep breath. "I can always tell when I have a fever. I just can't get warm enough. Isn't that funny? Your body is burning up, but you have the chills."

"Can I get you anything?"

"Dad has that homemade wine. I know it's early, but it sure sounds good"

"I'll get it." I stood and walked to the kitchen. The jug marked homemade wine was out on the counter. Seeing it made me smile. My father convinced everyone he made that wine himself. When it fact, he bought cheap grape wine, added grape vodka and soaked cherries in it for two weeks. People loved it.

I grabbed a glass and poured a healthy serving for my mother.

"Have you heard from Brad or Michael?" she asked.

"No," I replied and walked into the living room, handing her the wine. "Nothing. I'm not sure there is any service though." I returned to my seat on the coffee table. "Brad's been pretty good. Unless he ran into trouble or couldn't get a connection, I can't see him not calling. Michael ... I don't think he has a working phone."

"I'm so sorry." She took a good drink of the wine and complimented on how good it felt in her mouth.

"I am so sorry you're sick."

"There was no avoiding it."

"I doubt that. I think if you would have ..."

"No." She shook her head. "Going by what your father said before. If you're meant to get it you will. I was meant to get it."

"I wish Michael was here for you. I wish ... I wish he would have thought about us."

My mother shook her head. "You have to think of it another way. He's not here to see any of this. He'll face the aftermath, but that is easier than watching it happen."

I was ready to comment on that, how she was probably right, when my phone rang. I reached into my pocket for it, thinking it was Brad.

It was a number I didn't know.

"Who is it?" my mother asked.

"I don't know. But it's somebody." I pressed the button. "Hello."

I heard a weeping breath, followed by, "Mom."

"Michael." My eyes widened, I stood and looked at my mother.

"Mom. Mom, I'm so sorry. I'm so sorry I left. I should have told you," he wept as he spoke. "Sophia was sick. I didn't want you to say 'no'. I'm sorry …"

"Michael, no, it's fine. You're fine. That's what matters."

"I wanna come home. I just wanna come home."

"Where are you?" I asked.

"Pittsburgh."

Immediately I thought back to Ivy and how we were stuck like Michael at a medical camp. Unable to drive, or to move my truck. I thought about what my father did when I called, no hesitation to come. "Michael, where in Pittsburgh are you?"

"Um …" Then he spoke to someone, there was a man in the background. Michael asked where he was. I heard the response of 'North Shore Medical Camp.'.

"Did you hear that?" Michael asked.

"I heard. Michael, I'll be there. I'm on my way."

"Mom, they shut all the roads down, bridges too. I just want to come home and there's no way."

"Michael, it's Pittsburgh. You're on the north shore. Where?"

"Army tent by the stadium."

"Even better. I don't need a road. I have the river. Just ask that man if you can hold on to his phone or stay close to him in case I need to call."

"I have the phone. Some guy got arrested and he dropped it. I …. I called the last number he dialed to let them know. He was trying to get medicine. I wanted his family to know in case they were waiting."

"That was … that was really nice and smart. Michael, hang tight with the Army. I'm on my way. Okay? I'm on my way." As I went to hang up I heard Michael tell the person in the background that I was coming.

I put my phone back in my pocket, then I realized … my mother.

How was I supposed to leave her when she was sick?

"Clare ... is he alright?"

"I think. He's really upset." I started to dial the phone and call Brad. Maybe he was nearby or close enough to come to my house for my mother. The phone rang, but in the middle of the second ring, it did some sort of odd tone. "Damn it."

"It's a long distance on the river to Pittsburgh," my mother said. "You better go."

"Mom, I can't leave you like this. I just ..."

"You are a mother first," she said. "If it were me. I'd leave to get my child. Go. I'll be fine."

I leaned down to my mother and kissed her, then I went into the kitchen, grabbed that jug of wine and brought it close to her. "I'll be back."

"I know you will."

"I love you."

She smiled at me, reaching for my hand and squeezing it. "I love you, too." She paused. "Clare?"

"Yeah."

"I know you don't think it. I know you're waiting to get sick. I truly believe you have been spared. I really do. Just know, the world is a lucky place to have you left to build it again."

I closed my eyes tightly, trying not to cry. I mouthed the words 'I love you' again and then 'goodbye.'

It killed me to leave, in fact I walked backwards to the door, afraid to take my eyes off my mother. I hoped she would be alright and alive when I returned, but a part of me knew as I opened that door, that would be the final time I saw her face, or heard her voice.

I took one last look at my mother, closed the door and left so I could get my son.

THIRTY-TWO - THE CRANE

I sent a text to Brad. I didn't know if he would get it or not, but I had to try. I told him Michael was in Pittsburgh and I was on my way to pick him up. Could he please get back to Mills Run and sit with my mother?

If Michael was with the Army and they said all roads and bridges were closed, I had to believe them, or else my son would have been back home. We were fifty miles southwest of Pittsburgh. A good hour drive. However, that wasn't the case when taking the river. There were many things to consider. The Ohio River was a complicated water way with locks and dams and was far from a straight shot. It looped down and around like a horseshoe and was twice the distance in nautical miles.

While I could easily take the ferry, it would take forever. Top speed of the ferry was twenty knots and that was pushing it. I would burn through copious amounts of fuel. I needed another boat. No matter what I used, I had to maintain a good cruising speed and not push it. The river was unpredictable and I wasn't certain if any of the fueling docks would be operational without power.

Knowing the area as well as I did, having navigated up and down the Ohio, I knew what I needed and where to get it. Howard Larkin had a twenty-four foot Rinker Boat. He always topped off his tank at the Steubenville Marina before docking at the Mills Run shore. He hated fueling in the morning.

With a full tank of fuel I would be able to get to Pittsburgh and back if I didn't force the engine. I just needed his keys. I took the SUV and drove over to Howard's house. Apparently my father had marked the homes there. Houses on both sides of the two block street were spray painted and Howard's was no different.

The X on the house wasn't surrounded by a circle but rather a square.

Infected.

On the right side of the X was the number two. Howard and his wife, I assumed. That was two days earlier and I was certain, with this fever, Howard and his wife would be gone.

Out of respect, I knocked on the door, then knocked again and called out.

When I stepped inside, there was a slight odor of death. It wasn't overwhelming and that told me Howard and his wife were probably on the second floor, or behind a closed door.

"Howard?" I called out again.

No answer.

There was an eerie quiet to the home, not noise. The blinds and curtains were drawn and the first floor was dark. I opened them to add light so I could search for the keys. A stale smell of cigarettes lingered in the air as well. Howard's blue wind breaker jacket was tossed on the couch and on the coffee table was an open pack of cigarettes. In the ash tray was a cigarette that had burned completely away and was nothing but one long ash. Howard probably came in, dropped his coat, lit it, was too sick to smoke it and walked away.

Where would his keys be?

The kitchen was my first guess because it was where my father kept his. A boat key was slightly different and easy to spot. I only hoped the key was on the first floor, I hated the thought of looking for Howard and having to search his bedroom, or clothes.

Howard Larkin and his wife tried to fight the fever and remain strong.

On the stove was a small pot and next to it on the counter, an empty can of soup. Two bowls were on the table, and flies buzzed around the untouched liquid contents. One of those Sam's Club giant bottles of ibuprofen was open on the table. I began my search of the kitchen, looking in every drawer and cabinet along with visually scanning every inch of counter space.

I moved on to the dining room and did the same thing there. Nothing was found.

I still had the living room to check and that back room on the first floor.

I amped up my searching methods, moving more frantically, wanting to get out of there and needing to find those keys.

I was frustrated and angry. Where were they? Then I thought of that blue windbreaker.

Howard wore it when boating.

I rushed over to the coach, lifted the coat and when I did I heard the jingle. Reaching into the pocket, I felt the key chain and pulled it out. Sure enough, attached to a red anchor key chain was a boat key.

I clutched it in my hand. "Thank you, Howard" Then I left the house, making sure the door was closed behind me.

I drove down to the marina. Howard's boat was docked down river from the ferry. I paused to look at it. She was my father's pride and joy. He had done so much work on her, and put so much of himself into the ferry. I made a promise to myself, if I were to beat the fever then the ferry would be my pride and joy.

I boarded the boat and checked the fuel levels, as I suspected there was a full tank. Howard had thought like my father. He probably had a plan to leave or isolate himself. The boat was stocked with water and food.

By the time I was ready to cast off, it was pushing two PM. My goal was to be home by evening. I didn't want to navigate the Ohio in the dark. However, I didn't know what Pittsburgh would bring. There was a possibility the journey wouldn't be a quick one.

I set my course, turned on the radio, started the engine and left. I was hoping to hear some sort of chatter on my way, but I didn't. It was dead silent.

Even though Mills Run battled the fever virus and lost, there was still hope out there. Some of the bigger cities, like Pittsburgh, were still alive.

Maybe they knew something we didn't, or had a cure we didn't know about. It wouldn't be long before I found out.

I moved at a good speed, not too slow and not so fast that I was burning through the fuel.

Within twenty-minutes, I was passing Steubenville. I slowed down and lifted the binoculars. I didn't see any people walking around. Cars were stopped and crammed the roads. Many had doors left open and were abandoned.

I listened for any sounds of life. There wasn't a motor, horn, bird, nothing at all …Steubenville was still.

As was the river. It didn't have the usual current or movement. Usually an abundance of boats or barges moving caused a ripple effect, but there wasn't any. Just the lack of life on the Ohio River told me I wasn't going to spot many river travelers at all.

In fact, I remained the sole person on the river and spotted no other movement until after I went by East Liverpool and crossed into Pennsylvania. Things looked a little different.

Boaters have a different mentality, especially those who boat on the river. Most of the time, their lives revolved around how they would fit the boat into their plans. My father was the same way, even with the ferry.

His first mindset was survival and how he would work the ferry into it.

Judging by the cases of water and canned food on board Howard's boat, I was confident in believing he was thinking the same thing.

My father and Howard weren't the only ones.

I called it the horseshoe, it was a thirty mile stretch of river north of Pittsburgh. Once I hit that, I started to see my more life.

There were boats, most large, were anchored in the middle of the river. People moved about them watching as I passed.

One of the boats had drifted ashore, the man in the exposed captain's chair was slumped over at the wheel.

I thought of the families that took to their boats as a form of sanctuary. Get away from people, stay away. Stay alive. Seeing them made me think of everyone close to me I had lost.

I wondered if we had gotten on the ferry just a day earlier would my daughter, son and father be alive? Would my mother be ill? Or would we had been like the man slumped in the captain's chair, a mere victim no matter what he tried to do to escape the fever.

The man in the captain's chair more than likely died where he loved being.

Just as I thought about my father and how he always said, though illegal, he wanted his ashes placed in the river, I saw a body floating by.

It was wrapped in a black bag, it was followed by another then another. Were people that insensitive that they just placed the bodies in the water, where had they come from? A few miles down the river and many bodies later, I received my answer.

Like we were doing in Mills Run, the bodies were being placed onto barges. Whether it was the people of the small town of Ambridge doing so or the county, it was a mass river burial that failed. I watched as I passed, people in masks and hazmat suits were controlling the garbage style trucks. There were six trucks lined up.

My God, that many people? Like refuse collectors leaving garbage at the dump, the hiss of the air lift echoed as the workers lifted the back end and dropped the bodies over the edge of the wharf into the barges. It was hit and miss, some bodies bounced off and rolled into the river. The one barge was so full, that when the bodies rolled from the trucks, the large pile toppled, sending them into the river.

As cold as it seemed, it was the way of the world, the way it had to be.

How much more would be left when the workers died, when there weren't enough people to move the bodies?

<><><><>

I heard the sound of a dying city long before I even saw the crest of the Pittsburgh skyline. Thick black smoke lingered in the sky, and the continuous sounds of gunfire, sirens and explosions filled the air.

My heart raced out of control. My poor son, no wonder he sounded so scared.

I had made three river journeys to Pittsburgh in the years I had manned the ferry. It was only three. My father did the rest. It was enough times to let me know that everything had changed.

Pittsburgh was a city of bridges. Many bridges connecting the north and south to downtown, crossed the three rivers of the area.

One of those brides was a hundred year old landmark. That bridge, the West End, was gone. The ends of the bridge were burnt and broken, the center had toppled into the river. Some of it extended up. Slowly and carefully, I maneuvered through the wreckage. When I did, I saw the Fort Pitt Bridge, another artery to the city, was totally destroyed.

I was glad my destination was not downtown.

Pittsburgh was a warzone. It was in the middle of a battle and by what I could see, they fought diligently. My guess was that they, like everyone else ... were losing.

The north shore offered a devastating view of Pittsburgh. My first inclination was to dock at the center Market Street pier, but I opted against that because the river was filled with debris along with bodies and the farther I moved upstream the more chance I took of hitting something.

I steered over to the River Quest Dock. It was private and reserved for vessels affiliated with the museum on the North Shore. No one was there, and I felt it was safe, amidst the confusion and chaos. Since there was no boat traffic around, leaving would be easier.

I just had to find my son and go.

He said he was on the North Shore, with the Army near the stadium. There were two stadiums on the north side of Pittsburgh. To me, an Army set up would be easy to spot.

I docked the boat and secured her, keeping the keys, the last thing I needed was for someone to take the boat.

Finding Michael was my only focus. I had to ignore everything I heard and saw and just focus on my son. I checked my phone. While my battery was low, it was the strongest signal I had seen my entire trip. I immediately dialed the phone that Michael had called me from.

It rang four times and then the voicemail picked up. "Hey, this is Dodge, you know what to do. Leave ..."

I hung up and tried again. Again, it went to voicemail. Placing my phone in my pocket, I started to walk the pier when a soldier stopped me. He held a rifle, but not in a threatening manner to me and he only wore a mask.

"Ma'am, did you just come from that boat?" he asked.

"I did."

"This area is shut down. No one is permitted in."

"I need to find my son," I said.

"Ma'am this area is for drop off. Medical distribution is shut down."

I moved closer and he stepped back. "Please." I pleaded. "He came here. He brought his girlfriend. He's only a teenager. He called. He asked me to come get him. He said he was at an Army tent outside the stadium."

"I can't let you in the zone."

"I have come all the way ..."

"I'm sorry."

My anger grew and I grunted. "It doesn't make sense. Why is this closed? It's over, this thing beat us."

"We're still fighting it and things are out of control down this way. We have people dying from violence as much as the virus. It's for your safety as well," he said.

"I don't care about my safety." I snapped. Was this really happening? Did I leave my mother in search of my son only to be shut down? The world was on a fast track spiral and not only were there still ridiculous quarantine rules, but the young soldier was still holding post. He like my own son should have been with his family. I was certain he had a mother out there somewhere, worried and crying.

"Ma'am, I should detain you, but I'm not. I'm going to ask you to get back on your boat and go."

Through the tops of my eyes, I looked at him and softened my voice. "I am begging you. Begging, I lost my daughter, my other son, my father, my mother and my friends to this thing. He is all I have left in this world. Please, let me find my son. I just want to take him home."

I would have pleaded with him as a father, but he looked too young to have a child.

He lowered his head. "You said he was at the Army tent?"

I nodded. "Someone in the background told him where to tell me to go. They're watching out for him, I know it."

"That makes sense if he's at the tent. What's his name?" he slung his rifle over his shoulder and grabbed his radio. When he did I noticed the name on his Army Jacket. It was Stevens.

I exhaled loudly in relief. "Michael. Michael Gifford."

He nodded. "If he's not there and no one's seen him, you have to get back on the boat."

Hating to agree, I nodded. I'd find another way if I had to leave. Another pier, another soldier to argue with. I'd find a way.

"Sarge," he called into his radio. "Stevens here, you copy? Over."

"Copy. What's up? Over."

"Do you by some chance have a teenage boy named Michael Gifford in the tent? Over."

There was a pause.

"Who wants to know?"

"His mother. He called her and she came by boat. Wants to take him home. Over."

Another pause. "I know where he is. Bring her down. Over."

My breath shivered and my body trembled. He had Michael. I wanted to scream I was so relieved. "Thank you. Thank you so much."

"But, Sarge, the no entry order?" asked Stevens. "Over."

"She just wants to bring her son home. Not like she's staying, right? Let her get her son. Bring her down. Out."

Stevens hooked his radio. "He wants me to bring you to him."

"I heard. If you can't leave your ..."

"No. No." Stevens shook his head. "I'll take you. It's kind of crazy. That secure?" He pointed to the boat.

"It is."

"This way." He began to walk down the pier.

I followed.

He asked where I was from and I told him. Then he questioned how Mills Runs was faring.

"We're not," I answered. "A good bit of the town left to get help, the rest are either dead, or dying. We faded fast."

"No, that's most of the country. Some places were done weeks ago. Pittsburgh is one of the last places standing. Even that won't be for long. We lost control yesterday."

"You mean with the sick."

"No, that's been out of control for a while. I'm talking law and order .... Bodies."

I nodded my understanding. When we walked up the pier there was no one around. As soon as we emerged to the street level military trucks zoomed by, the backs of which were loaded with bodies.

People cried out, reaching for us, begging for help as we passed them by. They lined the streets, sitting on the ground, leaning against other dead bodies. Instead of dying in their home, they chose to seek help and hope and spend their final moments on a street corner alone. It was sad.

We weren't far from the stadium, and as we drew closer I saw the fence along with military tents erected outside the main gate. Then I saw something more horrifying than anything I had seen. It authenticated the reality of the virus and the dooming fate of mankind.

We were done. It was over. There was nowhere else to go.

The sight of it made me physically stop as I watched.

A huge crane lifted up and swung over the stadium, the large claws of the crane opened and out toppled bodies. Multitudes of bodies rained onto the grass , falling fast through the air to their final destination of the football stadium below. How many bodies were in there, how high was the pile inside? Once it released its load, it swung back down and dipped.

Within a minute, it repeated, dropping dozens more bodies into the stadium.

"Oh my God," I spoke near a whisper as I watched.

"It's the only place to put them," Stevens said. "The plan is to burn them. We're waiting on orders. It's nearly full."

"Full?"

"Local news claims about seventy thousand died from this virus. There's more, there's probably double that. At least from what I have seen here, it already is fifty thousand. That's just the stadium. You have PNC field that is full and the folks at home. See? We're not different from your Mills Run, just on a bigger scale."

He was right. Pittsburgh put their dead in stadiums, we put ours on a barge.

"Right there." He pointed to the first tent. "Wait here, I'll be right back."

He disappeared into the tent and a few moments later another soldier emerged and walked directly to me. This soldier was young as well, only he wasn't wearing a full face mask, just one of those paper ones.

"Mrs. Gifford?"

Correcting him and saying my last name was different than my sons, seemed inane at the time and I merely stated, "Clare."

"Clare, I'm Sergeant Wilkes. I was with Michael when he called you."

"Oh." I placed my hand to my chest as I breathed out. "Thank you so much for watching him and keeping an eye out."

"Ma'am, once he came to the tent, I need you to know he never left my sight. I was by him the whole time."

"And I thank you for that. He's so young. I know he comes across as mature, but he's still young. He had to be scared. Thank you again. Also, thank you for letting me come back here to pick him up."

Wilkes nodded.

"Is he coming out?" I looked behind him. "Or is he somewhere else?"

"I'll take you to him," Wilkes said. "But there's something I need to tell you. I ... he...." He paused. "I'm sorry."

"Excuse me?"

"This way." He turned without saying a word and walked to the tent.

With trepidation, I went with him.

A screaming, "No", repeated loud and long in my mind as I stared at the lifeless body of my oldest child. For the first few minutes of learning he was gone, my own voice blasted in my head. I cried out every word I could imagine that displayed my disbelief. I mentally screamed and cried so loud that I couldn't hear any other sounds. Yet nothing emerged from my mouth. The abundance of pain and hurt I felt at that moment left me with the inability to speak. I breathed out slowly, my slightly parted lips acted like a release valve. Almost as if the air was a thick residue of the pain, coating my lungs and being, trying to escape me anyway it could

My poor son. My poor boy. He was gone.

I embraced the joy of the day he came into my life and I would forever curse the agony of the day he left it. I was broken. The final straw. Crushed beyond believe. There was no way my heart would even begin to heal.

He had a special place in my heart in life and in death.

I knew it though. A part of me knew it the second Wilkes responded to Stevens with a delay. I didn't want to admit that something was wrong.

When he led me into the tent, a completely silent tent, my heart stopped.

Michael's body was on a cot, a body bag beneath him, yet he was covered with a blanket. I had to roll it down from his face to look, to make sure it was my son.

"Oh, baby." I stroked his face. "I am so sorry. I didn't even say 'I love you' when I hung up. I'm sorry."

"He knew," Wilkes said then cleared his throat. "He knew. Michael was a very smart young man. He was sick when I found him."

I listened to Wilkes, but my eyes didn't leave my son. "Where? Where did you find him? Please don't tell me he was laying on the road ..."

"No. No. He was caught up in the trouble at the medicine table. They stopped handing it out. People fought. I saw him and knew he wasn't part of it. So I pulled him out, it's when I saw he was sick. He was ... also pretty upset."

"Thank you for doing that."

"I can't image the pain you are feeling. I don't know if this helps but I didn't leave his side, not once. Okay? He wasn't alone. He told me about you, your father. Ivy and Eli..."

That was the first moment I looked at him. My lips puckered.

"He didn't leave this world alone. I thought .. you know..." Wilkes blinked slowly and held his eyes closed for a second. "I thought about my mom. About how she would feel if he were me and she was on her way. Truth is, I know how he felt. He was me. You're never too old to need your mom. I'm twenty-five. More than anything right now, I want to see my mother. I need to. This has to be killing her."

"It is." I wiped my eyes, kissed Michael's forehead and covered his face before I stood. "I'm sure she's proud of you and what you're doing. Know that. And she's thinking of you and she loves you. Right now, I'd love to hug you, but I understand if you ..."

The young man didn't wait for me to finish, he stepped to me and reached for that hug. Even though he was taller, I wrapped my arms around him in the most comforting and grateful way I could, my hand cupping the back of his head, pulling him to me as I would my own son. He needed that embrace, he was still so young. Even though he was in a uniform, serving his country, he was still a child.

He stayed in my arms for a small amount of time, then we both knew it was time to part. He had a job to do, one that was coming to an end and I already knew it would be dark by the time I got back to Mills Run.

Wilkes and Stevens carried my son back to the boat. I walked with them, my hand on Michael with each step we took.

They placed him carefully inside the boat and I thanked them both. After a short goodbye, I was on my way.

As much as I hated the outcome, I accomplished what I set out to do. I journeyed to Pittsburgh to get my son and bring him home. I was doing just that.

It wasn't what I hoped for, it wasn't what I wanted, it was what it was and I had to face it.

I thought of the woman I had met in Steubenville at the Medical Camp. Her son Danny had died and it was the fourth child she had lost.

That woman was strong and calm. In some ways I had become her. She wished me well and I remembered her words.

"It doesn't get any easier, it just absorbed into the numb and pain that's already there. You know?"

Sadly, as I traveled with my son's body ... I did know.

THIRTY-THREE - DARKEST NIGHT

I was grateful for the clear star filled sky and the bright moon or else I would have had to anchor for the night. Just after I entered the Ohio West Virginia area complete nightfall set in and things were dark. There were no street lights, no distance view of candles burning or fires ... nothing. It was complete and utter darkness. I relied on the spot light and the reflection of the moon as I navigated the river slowly.

It was a quiet lonely ride and then a few miles beyond Steubenville, I saw the dances of orange light.

I knew instantly it was coming from Mills Run and my initial fear was a fire. The closer I pulled, the more I could see they were tiki torches. Four of them were set up near the dock and in between, shining out, were high beam headlights from a vehicle.

The combination of them all lit the area enough for me to safely dock.

I couldn't see much behind the lights, it looked like a black wall. I pulled in, shut down the engine and began to tie up the boat when I heard footsteps on the pier. Looking up, I could only see a silhouette until Brad stepped even closer.

"You're alright," I said with some relief.

"I am. Your mom told me you took the boat to get Michael. I figured you needed light to dock."

"I did." I stepped on the dock.

"Where's Michael?"

Hands to my hips, I lowered my head and turned toward the boat.

Brad was confused at first, then he probably saw the body bag. "No, oh, Clare. I'm sorry."

"Me too. How ... how is my ..."

Brad shook his head. "She passed about two hours ago. She didn't suffer. She was good until the end."

"I'm glad you were there."

"I tried to get back to you. I couldn't. No clear signal so I hurried home," he said. "How are you?"

"Horrible. Done. I just want to get him home. Can you help?"

Brad didn't say anything, he just walked straight to the boat. Together we got Michael and placed him in Brad's truck. Then I walked over to get the SUV that was still parked by the dock.

Brad made it to my house first, when I arrived a few minutes later, he was already inside and had taken Michael to the back room.

The battery operated lantern was still on, so the house wasn't dark. It felt strange walking in. My home that always carried a sense of warmth just felt dead. My mother was on the couch, lying on side, her hand under a pillow with covers to her shoulders. I would had sworn she was sleeping had it not been for the deep discoloration on her face.

I said my goodbyes to her and thanked her, but for as horrible as it sounded, I couldn't stay in there. I just couldn't. Then again, I couldn't leave. So I moved the SUV as close to the porch as I could and sat there watching the house.

Brad left, he only waved at me when he did. Then he returned a half hour later and knocked on the passenger door.

I waved for him to get inside.

"I won't stay long," he said, sliding in. "I just ...." He put a bottle of water on the seat and sandwich. 'I figured you didn't eat. The bread won't be fresh much longer so eat up. I know you aren't feeling hungry but you need to eat. Also ..." He placed a bottle of whiskey on the seat. "In case you want a drink."

I nodded then looked at what he brought. I grabbed the bottle, opened it and took a drink. I showed it to Brad.

"No, I'm good. I ... I made rounds while waiting on you. Maybe a few are still alive, they're sick though. I'm not thinking long term right now, I am thinking about my father."

I looked at him.

"Tomorrow I am going to Steubenville. I know the roads are blocked, but there's a mass grave site on the outskirts I can get to. I'm going to steal one of the mini excavators they have. Hitch a trailer to my truck. Get it here. If that doesn't work, or I can't get that, I may need to find one. I just want you to know where I'll be in case it takes me awhile. I have to bury my father, Clare. He deserves a proper grave." He exhaled. "Everyone does. I don't have it in me to do that for everyone. There are those I want to do it for. Sam, for one."

"Have you seen him?"

Brad nodded. "I stopped in. He was in his office, head on the desk, bottle still in his hand. He passed that way."

"I think getting one is a good idea. I don't imagine I have the strength to dig graves."

"Are you sick?"

"No. Unfortunately." I shook my head. "I'm still physically fine. Will you bring it here when you're done with your father?"

"Absolutely, I will. What are you going to do tonight?"

"Tonight ..." I sighed. "I'll sit here. Pull a Sam. Drink until I'm numb. Try to sleep. When I get up, I'll start getting things prepared in the yard. I just don't know if I am ready yet to face the fact I need to bury my entire family."

"Whenever you're ready, I'll help."

"I know. Thank you."

"Did you need me to stay here? Keep you company?"

I shook my head. "No, I need to be alone." I chuckled emotionally. "Odd huh. I need to be alone when right now, I am absolutely alone in this world."

"No you're not." He stared at me.

I returned to looking at the house.

"I'll let you be. I'll find you when I get back." He opened up the door. "Goodnight, Clare."

"Goodnight, Brad."

The door shut, I took another swig from the bottle and sat back, elbow on the doorframe, my head resting in my hand.

I didn't know how to even process the massive amount of thoughts I was having, or the incredible amount of grief that swallowed my soul.

My family was gone.

Life would be different. The thought of life was a joke to me. It was inconceivable that there was anything after the death of Michael. Nothing was left. To me the notion of there being another page in my life book, of there being a tomorrow was hard to believe. It was over, right? How could I live another day? How could I go on? The awful truth was, the sun would rise the next day, the world would go on and unless I died in my sleep, I would have to go on with it.

THIRTY-FOUR - THE SHOVEL

April 28

Too much loss, too much pain, no sleep for two nights, and a half a fifth of whiskey left me at a wall of exhaustion I was unable to break through. Staring at the house, I fell asleep with my hand on the steering wheel and a bottle between my legs. I woke up the same way. Somehow, though, I sat up quickly, expecting things to be different. The hard-hit to my stomach was a message of reality that everyone was gone. My entire family was gone.

My home which usually looked bright and welcoming, looked dark and dreary under the overcast sky. My intention was to stay in the truck until Brad returned. That would be my sign to get moving. As the storm rolled in I had a feeling Brad wasn't going to be returning as soon as I expected. By late morning, it started to rain. It poured down so hard, and beat so loudly against the truck there were times where I had to shield my ears. But that didn't change anything. I still stayed right there Crying, thinking, then crying again.

I wanted my children to be alive, I wanted so badly for them to run from the house.

They didn't.

I didn't move from the SUV. The only time I stepped out was when I had to use the bathroom. It wasn't often. And because I could not bring myself to walk through my front door, I used the neighbor's house. I knew they weren't there.

As I thought, Brad didn't come back that night. I didn't worry, I knew it was too dark and dangerous to travel.

My day was a repeat of the night. Sitting in the truck, staring at the house, crying and thinking, trying not to picture my children without life.

The storms stopped and the sun rose the next day.

I woke up feeling horrible.

This is the day I get sick and die, I thought.

That wasn't the case. I hadn't eaten and was living off whiskey and the single bottle of water Brad had given me. My body was weak and dehydrated.

Sitting there and doing nothing was a disservice to my family. They deserved more than to remain in the house covered in blankets. The ground was wet and soft from the storms, I could get things started before Brad returned, but first, I had to get myself together.

My family was in the house.

No, wait, not my entire family. Ivy was missing. Before I did anything, I had to go to Feeny's and get Ivy.

When I went to retrieve her I wanted to do so with dignity, that meant washing my face, changing my clothes. For the sake of Ivy, I would walk into Feeny's and at least look as if I were keeping it together.

Truth was, I wasn't. I was falling apart.

I parked the SUV so close to the house, that all I had to do was open the door and step out and I was on the porch. I moved slowly and apprehensively, as if I were afraid with every step I took. I walked up to the porch, opened the screen door, then reached for the main door. Slowly I turned the knob. The moment I broke the seal and the door opened ever so slightly, a wave of horrible stench hit me and I quickly pulled the door closed. I spun around and raced to the railing, trying to catch my breath and stop myself from gagging. I was sick to my stomach, not because of the smell, but because of what was happening to my family. What I allowed to happen. My father, my mother, my sons. All of them in a decomposing state because of my cowardice and inability to deal with it. The thoughts of the smell I decided right then and there, I was ending it. They deserved more than to rot on a couch. It was a dishonor to let them stay in that house any longer. The next time I entered that house, it would be to get them, to bring them out, and put them to rest.

Again, I used the neighbor's house. This time to clean up. In the basement I found some clothes that were freshly folded on top of the dryer. I used water from the water heater to wash up and I got myself together. I left a note for Brad on my front porch that I was leaving, just in case he got back before me. Without hesitation I got in the SUV and headed to get Ivy.

On the way, I pulled over at the Stop and Go convenience store. Of course, it was closed. The door was broken. I wasn't the first to go in there. I was hungry and I needed to get something in my stomach. The shelves were half bare. I managed to grab a bottle of cola, a package of HoHos, a carton of cigarettes and three lighters. I hadn't smoked in years. I didn't know whether or not I would start again. Perhaps deep down subconsciously I was thinking if I picked up the habit, it would quicken my route to seeing my children. Obviously, the fever wasn't getting me. I was angry about that.

I finished the cakes pretty quickly. In fact they caused a knot to form in my stomach. I suppose the cola broke it down. After I had consumed some sugar and energy I continued on.

The remaining trip to Weirton was uneventful. I knew the bridge to take, the back roads to drive, all of which took me to Feeny's without going near the heart of downtown. Fortunately, Feeny's was located on the outskirts. However by the amount of abandoned cars outside of Feeny's, had I not known better I wouldn't have sworn Feeny's was in a business district. Even though I doubted someone was going to pull in behind me, I had learned my lesson in Steubenville and parked a block down the road.

There was no one around. No sounds, no people. As I passed each car, I looked inside. They were empty, some doors were left wide open. They probably came to Feeny's to drop off or pick up somebody, and like me in Steubenville were blocked in.

Like many others, Feeny's was once a big old Victorian house converted to a funeral home. They had been in business for fifty years. They were trusted in the area, affordable, and they did a great job. Although they had a reputation for not doing the greatest of makeup, Feeny's cared. No one, no deceased family member was just another number to Feeny's. It was evident they cared because they went above and beyond to take care of the dead during the fever, long after everyone else had given up on cremating bodies.

The entrance doors to Feeny's were wide open and it looked dark from where I stood. It looked empty and abandoned. Despite the open entrance, I made my way around the side of the building, to the receiving doors. That was where I had been told to retrieve Ivy's ashes. When I got there I saw a sign hanging on the door which read, "All of your loved ones are in the coffee room. We did the best we could. We tried. Godspeed."

I reached out anyhow and tried those double doors. They were locked so I made my way around to the front of the building. Drawing closer to the main entrance, I could see the flies darting in and out. I knew what that meant. I came prepared and pulled a face mask from my back pocket, and from my shoulder bag I lifted a bottle of Febreze. I squirted it generously on the outside and placed it over my nose and mouth. It was a bit much. Overwhelming more like it. It would have to do. I would have to focus on the smell of the flowers in that air freshener because I knew what was ahead.

As soon as I stepped inside, the pungent smell in the funeral home cut its way through my scented mask. It was so strong my eyes watered and even though the deodorizer helped, it wasn't enough. I had to focus on not inhaling through my nose. The buzz of the flies was overwhelming. There had to be tens of thousands of them, if not more. The insect noise formed a steady loud buzz, like a running motor.

From where I stood I could see in the first viewing room. It was filled with bodies on tables. All of them covered, all of them still with their intake sheet propped on top. My footsteps disturbed the flies and immediately they pummeled at me. Darting in and out at me, trying to land, attacking me as if I were the new fresh meat. I just pushed through trying to find the coffee room. In my short journey through the lobby, I had to pass the children's room. When I did, I froze. It too was filled. Only there were more bodies, all of them small. My heart sunk. *Please*, I thought, *please don't let Ivy be one of those bodies. Please.*

I didn't want to leave her in the first place. I had felt guilty walking out. Now the thought she could still be there all these days later tore me apart.

I couldn't let those desperate thoughts consume me. Not yet. I had to look for the ashes first.

The coffee room was in the back of the building, it was more so a kitchen. I remembered it from the one time I had come to Feeny's for a funeral. When I stepped in there I was overwhelmed. Jars, containers, boxes, lined up everywhere. Every inch of counter and every table was covered with the ashes of those they cremated.

Before I even wondered how I'd find Ivy, I saw her. It was a beacon of light in the midst of the dark. Even in the middle of many others, I spotted that flip top mason jar.

Not only had Feeny's taken the time to put a pink ribbon on the jar, they placed her name on it and laminated her first grade picture on the front. It was the picture I had given them.

How very special they made that simple jar.

I whimpered, grabbed it and cradled it to my chest. I had her, my baby. Even though I wore a mask, I brought my lips to the lid.

I turned to leave and that's when I spotted the name on the small silver box.

Daljit Singh.

Sam's father.

He, like my family, needed to be buried. I couldn't leave him behind. Sam would want me to take the ashes, so I did.

It wasn't easy leaving Feeny's. I couldn't get all those people out of my mind. Those who remained unclaimed probably forever. They would be left there as their final resting place. The poor souls that were dropped off and never touched as it became too much for Feeny's because they probably caught the fever.

It was insane what happened to the world.

I wasn't alone in my pain.

Countless other parents were out there burying their children wishing it were them.

The death toll from the fever was extinction level. Like the Justinian Plague it would be a blurb in a history book thousands of years down the road. A massive historical event that went unheard of because no one was around to record it and even more so, no one was around to read it.

Everything was embedded in my mind. I wasn't the one who would pass the story on. God willing, burying my family would be my final chapter and I'd close the book on my life.

I placed Ivy and Sam's father both on the front seat and secured them with the belt. The entire ride home I talked to them both, telling them all about what happened as if they were actual passengers.

Brad still hadn't returned when I arrived, I figured it wouldn't be long.

I couldn't go in the house, not yet. I planned on waiting for Brad to help me. In the meantime, I would start preparing the back yard. Figure out where I wanted to place the graves, possibly even leaving room for my own.

We had a detached garage, but we never used it for vehicles. My father kept his tools in there and I grabbed the spade shovel. It wasn't my intention to dig, just to clean and make it nice.

Our back yard wasn't small, but it wasn't huge either. A good quarter of it was the back driveway my father had built.

We didn't have a garden, just some bushes and I thought about where the graves would go. Near the house, or at a distance. I needed enough space for six graves, although I wasn't sure if I was going to bury Ivy. I debated on just marking a grave and holding on to her ashes. Especially since Feeny's took such care.

I decided the best place would be in the far left corner of the yard near the fence. Brad could bring the excavator around the driveway and the area was easy for him to get to. Plus, I could block it off with flowers and make it nice. When I ventured to that corner, I realized when I started to mark the area that even though the ground was soft, there were a lot of rocks. Some of them were deep and the spade shovel wasn't going to work. I needed something heavier.

Toting the spade, I walked around to the front of the house, and as I hit the edge of the porch, through the corner of my eye I caught the figure of a man.

I was not expecting to see anyone. I backed up so as not to be seen and clenching that spade shovel, I peeked around the house.

It couldn't be.

There had to be a mistake.

It was Sam. Was I hallucinating? Sam had died.

His back was to me and he was oblivious to everything, he staggered as he walked, dragging his foot along as his arm swayed back and forth lifelessly.

"Oh my God," I whispered.

Immediately, I grew fearful, certain the virus mutated and now my dear friend Sam was nothing more than a walking corpse. A zombie.

I wanted to scream, run into the house and get the gun, but Sam turned around and looked at me. He lifted his arm and took a step. Surely he was ready to attack. I didn't know if he was one of those fast moving dead, or the slow type. I couldn't take a chance. Not that I wanted to live, but I certainly didn't want to reanimate.

In a state of panic, I raised that spade shovel and, screaming out, I raced his way. I lifted it up high to strike him.

Sam stepped back and raised his arm. "The fever didn't kill me, but if you hit me with that, you will."

"Sam." I gasped out in shock, the shovel toppled from my hand and I immediately reached for him. "Oh my God, you're alive. You're alive," I gushed.

His eyes rolled to the back of his head as he groggily said, "Barely." Then his legs gave out and Sam fell to the ground.

THIRTY-FIVE – LOTTERY

For the time being, even if it was momentarily, I had a reprieve from the hurt and pain of death.

Sam.

After helping him stand, I walked over to Janice Belsterling's house next door. A cute cape cod that had previously been my go to wash room. Janice had left days before the fever piqued in Mils Run and never returned.

Her home would do. I didn't know much about Janice, she kept to herself, lived alone and worked outside of Mills Run. Her home was neat and tidy and she had an above average amount of food for a single woman. Most of it was ready made meals and cans of soup.

When my father had set up our camp on the front porch, he had a Coleman stove, I retrieved that and water and made Sam a cup of tea. He sat on the couch, a blanket over his shoulders, the box of his father's ashes on his lap as he cradled that mug in his hands.

He didn't look well. His face was exceptionally pale and his eyes were dark. I offered him some ibuprofen which was about the extent of my medical care.

"I'm fine," he said. "Just weak." He sat back. "Thank you. Thank you for getting my father's ashes."

"I saw them and I had to." I sat next to him. "Sam... how? How are you alive?"

"I don't know. I can't answer."

"I mean ... last I spoke to you, you were listening to Sixpence None the Richer ready to hook yourself up to a nonstop drip to death with Jack."

"That I can answer. I passed out before I hooked up the IV. Good thing huh?" He sipped the tea.

"Did you have the fever, or was it only a cold?"

"It was the fever. My nose was bleeding, my ears. I just ... I just recovered."

I nodded knowingly. "The one in the million."

"Remember I told you there are some people who would recover for some reason. I just never thought it would be me."

"What do you remember?" I asked.

"Being really drunk. I mean .. eyes rolling, everything spinning ... drunk. I put my head on the desk and I was out. I dreamt though ... weird dreams. I was listening to Sixpence and talking to Jim and Jack."

"Who?"

"Jim Beam and Jack Daniels. The men though. The real people."

"They aren't real."

Sam scoffed. "Sure they are. Jack's real name is Jasper. I know them well. In my dream they were my best buddies."

"I have news for you, Sam, they're your best buddies when you aren't dreaming. What did you talk about?"

"I don't remember. I know Brad was in my dream. Just briefly. He called my name, then said he was glad Jack was with me, or something like that and left."

"Brad checked on you. He said you were dead."

"I probably looked it. Next thing I know, I woke up and it was silent. I mean scary silent. I went to find you."

"It's been over two days."

"Holy shit. Two days," Sam exclaimed. "No wonder I pissed myself."

"It's a good thing Brad didn't put you ..." That thought made me gasp. "Oh my God. What if we buried people that were going to recover? What if we cremated them? What if we thought they were dead and they weren't. Like you."

Sam shook his head. "No, most everyone wasn't moved for days after they died. They would have gotten up. Even Feeny's had a three day wait. I think Feeny's would know if a person was dead or not."

"How?"

"Clare, they would be cold. They would discolor. This isn't an undead epidemic. I didn't die and rise, I was really sick and got better."

"We didn't wait to bury Jael. I took Ivy ..."

"Both of them ..." Sam held up his hand. "Their body temperature dropped. They had rigor mortis, meaning the blood settled to the bottom on them both. They weren't alive."

"I wish they were."

Sam looked down to the box of ashes. "Me, too. So ... have you heard from Michael?"

"He made it to Pittsburgh to get help for Sophia. I had to go get him. He ... he died."

Sam closed his eyes tightly. "Your mom?"

"They're all dead." I stood. "Hence, why you're here. I haven't been able to move their bodies from my house."

"I can help."

"No, you can't. Brad will help me. I want you to rest and get strong. I don't want you having a relapse. I need you to get well."

"Where is he?"

Just as Sam asked that question, I heard the sound of a motor pulling closer. "That's him now. Stay put, I'll be back." I walked from the living room out the front door and saw Brad pulling into my driveway.

His mission was to get a mini excavator and sure enough, he toted one on a trailer attached to a truck.

Stepping from Janice's porch, I moved across the lawn.

Brad got out of the truck and immediately went to the back to untie the excavator, as he did, he saw me and stopped. He turned from the trailer and walked my way.

I stopped on the edge of Janice's property.

"You look better," he said. "I'm sorry it took so long. I had to find another truck, the road washed away..."

"It's fine. It is. I needed the extra day." I looked back at Janice's house then to Brad.

"What's going on?"

"You were wrong."

"About?"

"Sam. You were wrong. He passed out drunk, some sort of recovery sleep, I suppose. He's not dead."

"Whoa. Wait. He had the fever."

"He did." I nodded.

"He's alive? He beat it?"

"Yeah, Sam beat it. He's inside sipping tea and recuperating."

Brad genuinely smiled and it was absolutely fine that he did so. Despite the deaths, the tremendous amount of suffering, and after all the darkness there was a speck of light. Instead of tears there was finally something to smile about.

THIRTY-SIX – FAR CORNER

April 30

We buried my family in a single afternoon, then Brad's father, Helen Jacobs and a few others from town. Sam placed his father next to mine and we agreed that after we finished with all the bodies in town, we would mark the graves permanently. Until then, we used a stake with a white cloth attached. Except for Ivy. I would mark a grave, but I couldn't bear to bury that jar, I couldn't part with it. I decided I would keep it, and in a sense always have a part of my baby girl with me.

One thing was for certain, since Sam's reprieve, Brad and I handled the bodies of our neighbors a lot differently. We checked them to make sure they had passed away. Twice I caught Brad looking over mounds he had stacked days earlier. Probably watching for movement, listening for sound. We had to be sure.

For two days we worked nonstop. It was better that way. Staying busy kept my mind off of my overwhelming grief. While Brad and I worked hard on getting the dead from their homes, Sam worked on etching our family's names in flat stones.

We didn't want him doing much. He was still sick and he lacked energy and strength.

Though we got a good bit of the houses cleaned out, we still had the bulk of Mills Run to do. It would take more than a few days.

The process would be a long one and unfortunately, it was just the beginning.

<><><><>

I had never heard of a tactical flashlight until Brad brought two back after his run. Those things were awesome. They extended a good five hundred feet and it wasn't just a beam, the flashlight brightened an entire area. It really helped while walking the dark streets of Mills Run.

Of course, the lights from the Pepper Mill flowed out into the street as well. Sam, even though still unwell, was back to his old habit and seated at the bar. Who were we to question whether it was a good thing for him to do, he was the doctor.

With a drink in front of him at the bar, Sam held a screw driver and worked on etching a name in the flat rock. "After this, I'll fill it in with some outdoor paint," he told us. "It'll look nice."

"Thank you both," I said, pouring a small drink. "Thank you for what you have done for my family."

"Thank you as well," Brad said, then placed his hand on Sam's back. "How are you feeling?"

"Better. I feel comfortable here. I don't have a home in Mills Run," Sam replied.

"You're welcome to stay with me," Brad told him. "I'm at my fathers."

"Or Janice's," I suggested. "It's nice there."

Sam shrugged, then blew the stone dust from the rock. "What about you, Clare? Your family is out of the house, it's been airing all day. You going to go back in there? I'm sure you need clothes."

"I don't know. I don't know if I'm ready. I may stay on the ferry. I know I have to rest. We have a busy day tomorrow."

"What's the plan?" Sam asked.

I looked at Brad, feeling funny about saying it out loud. "We're going to burn the bodies in the piles and on the ones on the barge."

"Too many flies," Brad said. "I also saw a couple of rats. We still don't know if Clare is immune, or just escaped catching it. We have to be careful."

"Do you plan on doing all the bodies in town?" Sam asked.

I replied, "Yes. The people of this town were amazing and I don't want them left in their homes like some sort of Omega Man, I am Legend movie. I want to clear Mills Run. It may take a while, but where else do we have to go, or do?"

Both Sam and Brad looked at me as if my saying that was insane.

"What?" I asked. "What else is there to do?"

"Options are endless," Brad said. "It's a big world. An empty one. Yours to explore. Hell, that Ferry is stocked. You could take it down the Ohio to the Mississippi, look for survivors and float on into the Gulf. Hit Florida keys. So much. We don't know what's beyond our west Virginia, Ohio circle."

"There's no reason to," I replied. "Everything just happened. Everything just ended."

"Doesn't mean we can't plan ahead," Brad said. "We're talking about cleaning Mills run."

"That's different. This is where I live and where I'll stay."

"You're staying here?" questioned Sam.

"Why does that surprise you? This is my home."

"Well, I can see if Brad said that. I mean, he was born here, lived here. You moved here like five years ago. I don't have enough fingers and toes to count how many times you said you wanted to leave. How you would go back to Nashville in a heartbeat if it wasn't for your father."

"I did say that but ... I can't go now. I just buried my entire family in my father's backyard. We're creating a cemetery for them. How can I leave? They're here."

"So, what I hear you saying is," Sam lifted his glass. "When you bury someone you love in a location, you should stay there?"

"I guess." I shrugged.

"Poor Jason must be pissed." Sam took a drink.

"What was that?" I asked in shook.

Brad shook his head and reached for the bottle. "Ah, man, low blow to talk about her husband."

"I'm just saying." Sam lifted his hand. "Jason is buried in Nashville. She left him."

"I go back and visit his grave once a year."

"You can do that here, too. Come back and visit their graves," Sam said.

"Why are you hell bent on me leaving?" I asked.

"Because you didn't get sick, you didn't catch the fever, I don't think you will," Sam said. "I want you to live."

"I won't if I stay here?"

"Nope." Sam shook his head. "No you won't. It's full of memories that will drive you insane instead of helping you. Your grief is huge, staying here will remind you of it. I know you, Clare, you're so strong, but staying in Mills Run won't want to make you keep going, it won't make you want to feel alive. It will slowly kill your soul"

"I have news for you, Sam." I took a small drink. "Nothing will make me want to keep going, to feel alive again. Nothing will."

"Quiet," Brad cut me off.

"What the hell?" I snapped.

"Shut up. Both of you. One second." He stepped away from the bar.

I should have known Brad would hear it first. He was in the mode, I knew it, always listening and he heard it. Then so did I, then Sam.

A baby's cry.

All of us jumped and ran outside.

Brad tossed me a tactical flashlight. "Where is that coming from?"

I listened. The tiny wail that sounded shrill and pain filled, cut through the night air. "I don't know," I said.

"Think. Think." Sam looked at me. "Who in town had a baby?"

My mind raced, I started to run through residents I saw, those I just heard about. Stuttering, I answered. "The Pearson's on Rose have a two year old."

"Does that sound like a two year old?" Brad asked. "The baby sounds young."

Newborn, newborn, I thought. "I don't know. Maybe it was someone at the hotel."

Sam asked. "Do either of you remember seeing a baby, grabbing a baby?"

I shook my head.

Brad moved about the street. "Come on. Come on, where are you coming from?'

"Split up, "Sam suggested. "We just split up and start looking that's the only ..."

"Oh my God," Brad said. "It's coming from down there." He pointed toward the river.

"Are you sure?" I asked.

Brad took off running. I hurried and followed him with Sam right behind me. He was right, the closer we got to the river, the louder the cry. It was also clear that the cry was slightly muffled.

The river meant one thing ... that baby was on the barge. We just put a lot of bodies in there. How did we miss a baby?

"It's in here." Brad aimed his light on the barge.

The site and smell of the barge filled with bodies was overwhelming. Where was the baby? How would we even find it.

Quickly, I handed my flashlight to Sam, took a breath as if I were going to swim, and climbed on the barge. The resting flies stirred up and they whipped into the air. I swatted them. Keep the light on this." I instructed, then called out. "Keep crying. I hear you. Keep crying."

It was impossible to move. The stench was too much and I kept fighting the gag that crept up in the back of my throat. Every step I took, it seemed I moved on a decomposing body. Some were hard, some squished as I placed my foot. I listened for the cry that started to weaken.

"I'm losing him," I said.

"This way," Brad called out.

I turned my head and he too, was in the barge, only on the other side.

"The baby is this way."

Being careful where I stepped, I climbed over the bodies and made my way to him.

"Don't move. Don't make a sound," Brad said. "Listen."

We were close, I could tell. The baby was somewhere.

Sam held the one flash light, it brightened the barge, but Brad pulled out the other and slowly scanned the bodies.

"The baby can't be buried. Or at least not deep," Brad said. "The weight on top would have killed him or her. Just look."

It seemed like it was taking forever, the cry weakening as we pretty much were searching for a needle in a haystack. The hidden picture, our own post plague called, 'Where's Waldo'.

Then finally, I saw movement. Just a slight movement. Grabbing Brad's flashlight I aimed the beam to the corner and saw the movement again.

A tiny hand.

Both Brad and I raced over, sure enough when we arrived, we saw only a part of the face peeking out from under an arm.

The child was so tiny, it was sheer luck, or maybe even the grace of God that I spotted the baby. I lunged that way, whipping the body from on top of him and reached down.

Before I lifted him, I realized how young he was and I carefully cradled my hands under his body and head.

He squirmed and cried out and the second he did, I whimpered and brought him into the folds of my arms.

I didn't know how to act, what to do, or even if I could move.

In the middle of all the death, all those bodies, we found a tiny speck of life.

I wasn't even sure if that was a good thing, because looking at him, seeing how weak and white he was, I didn't know at that moment if the infant would live or die.

THIRTY-SEVEN - ALONE

Even with Mills Run being as small as it was, for the life of me I couldn't remember who had a newborn. Brad suggested it was maybe someone visiting or staying at the hotel. He didn't even remember seeing a baby, let alone putting one on the barge.

The baby boy, whom we estimated to be no more than six weeks old, wasn't healthy at all. Sam couldn't determine if he was recovering from the fever, or if he had just come down with it. He had a temperature and was dehydrated.

Even more so, he was hungry.

Brad raced to the pharmacy to get a can of formula and a bottle while I helped Sam.

We had to search every drawer and the supply room until we found a catheter small enough for a child.

Poor Sam was beside himself trying to figure out where to run the line. Even though the boy stopped moving much, I held him still while Sam searched out a vein. He ended up going in the foot and creating a splint so he wouldn't kick it out.

It was a time will tell situation, the child was fevered, his lungs were fluid filled and wet sounding. It was terrifying and sad.

Brad returned with formula, a few tee shirts, diapers for the baby, and other baby items. While I made a bottle, I sent Brad up to Janice' house to get the Coleman stove. When he returned, I heated some water and wiped down the baby. He was covered with dirt and body fluids that weren't his.

The entire situation was just another crack in my already broken heart. That poor baby was amongst the dead and a mere twelve hours from being set aflame.

All of us were an emotional mess over it.

Sam tried to stay realistic. I tried to stay distant and Brad was hopeful, overdoing it because he blamed himself for the child being overlooked.

"What do we do now?" I asked, after I finished washing the baby.

"We wait." Sam told us. "That's all we can do. I don't think this little one is going to make it though. It would take a miracle."

"We've already had some the last two days," Brad said. "I think we'll see another."

I glanced at him wondering what he meant.

"Sam was a miracle," Brad said. "Us hearing and finding this baby ... was a miracle. If he wasn't meant to live than we never would have heard his cry. I believe that. I'll stay right here with him, if you guys don't want to. Just tell me what I need to do, Sam. I'll stay."

"Please don't think I'm cold," I said. "I'm going to leave. I can't watch another child die. I can't. I'm sorry."

I reached down to the baby, but curled my fingers and withdrew my hand before touching him, then I walked away.

The entire walk back to my house, my only thought was of that baby. Was I selfish for not wanting to be there with him. Just after I said I didn't think there was a reason for me to want to live again, we heard the baby cry. For a second, just a second, I thought God was saying, 'Here, here's a reason."

It wasn't the case. It was a cruel trick. There was no looking to that baby as a reason to live, not when he was going to die.

I made it all the way to the front door of my house, yet, I still couldn't go inside. I grabbed a lantern, sleeping bag, Ivy's ashes and walked to the back of the house.

I made camp near their graves, sat up and talked to them. Neither Sam or Brad came by, I figured the baby passed away and they didn't want to tell me.

After a while of talking, staring and thinking of my children, I lay down on the sleeping bag on my side, Ivy's ashes were on my left, just where my daughter always slept next to me. I rested my hand on the jar. It was the closest I could get to being near her, and then like that, under the star filled sky, I closed my eyes and tried to sleep.

THIRTY-EIGHT - NEXT

May 1

The quiet, warm morning caused me to stir. I looked at my watch and couldn't believe I had slept as long as I did. No one was around, just me outside sleeping on the ground. I never shut off the lantern and the battery had died.

I gathered my things and Ivy and started to go into my home. Again, I only made it so far. It was the day though, I would go in my house. It had been long enough.

The hours that were ahead of me were going to be long and hard. It was the day we were going to burn the bodies. There were still so many in town and in the houses, first we had to finalize the ones we stacked in mounds and on the barge.

I went over to Janice's house, washed my face and brushed my teeth. I needed coffee, but forgot my Coleman stove was still at Quick Med. I actually debated on getting a good cup of coffee by going to the ferry, firing her up and plugging in the pot. Instead, I opted for one of those cans of double strength coffee. It did the trick. After I got dressed and ate some crackers, I headed down to the wharf. I didn't see any smoke in the sky, so I knew Brad had not started burning.

Before I did anything, I wanted to check on Sam. Hopefully, he was feeling better.

When I made it to the river, I stopped to look at the ferry. I really needed to take her out. For the sake of my father, I couldn't let that ferry just sit.

I stood there for a while, sipping my coffee from a can.

"Morning." Sam approached.

"Morning. How are you feeling?" I asked.

"Better. Much better. I have some strength. I ate soup."

"Good. I don't need you leaving me again." I nudged my shoulder into him. "Brad and I have this today. I want you to relax."

"I will." He exhaled. "You didn't ask."

I turned and looked at him. "I don't want to know."

"You should. His fever is gone. He's been crying and eating. Heart is strong. Breathing is good. What a difference. He needed those fluids. I think we saved him."

"Really?" I asked with some enthusiasm.

"Yes. So you can stop pretending you don't care."

I lowered my head some. "I'm not an uncaring person. You know that."

"You're grieving, Clare. We all are," he placed his hand on my back. "I'm going to go get back to Baby Joe."

"You named him Joe?"

"Yeah, sure, why not. It's easy. I'll send out Brad." Sam started to walk away. "Hey, make sure Brad stops and eats today. I know he's not been doing that. We don't need him to drop on us."

I nodded my agreement, but thought it was a ridiculous request. Brad was a grown man. Sam was right however, we were all that was left. Whether we liked each other or not, we still needed to watch out for one another.

<><><><>

"What do you think it would take to plan long term survival?" Brad asked. It was an odd question, out of the blue, considering the first two hours of our day was spent double checking Rose street through Martin for bodies. They would be the last bodies we retrieved for the day, checking them for decomposition. Making sure they weren't in some sort of healing coma.

We washed up afterward, taking a break before we undertook the task of burning the bodies. I think unspoken, we were both procrastinating doing that. Like a mother hen with Sam's voice in the back of my head, I made Brad eat.

Our lunch was boxed cereal and peanut butter on crackers. Maybe it was the meal that made him think of long term survival.

"I mean," Brad looked at the peanut butter. "This is well and fine, but it can't be our way of life. We can't be like the movies scavenging for food. Right?"

"I guess. I mean there's a ton out there you know."

"I know. But like gasoline, it will eventually go bad. I want to be in a position where I'm getting ready to be self-sufficient before the food goes bad."

"Then you know your answer," I said. "Be self-sufficient for long term survival."

"What would it take? I can handle things just me, but now ... Joe is involved. How do you handle long term survival plans for an infant."

"Babies need fed and loved, as long as someone is there to do that, they'll go with the flow. Joe will adapt the easiest. He'll grow up in this world. He'll be smarter than us, I can tell you."

"You think?"

I nodded. "Yeah, plus, I don't think long term should be labeled 'survival', I mean if you're in it long term, you already survived. Take a look at my fath ,..." I choked on the word. "Father. He packed that ferry for survival, but he didn't think long term."

"Maybe he knew."

"Maybe."

"I just ..." He finished his cracker, dusted off his hands and stood. "I just worry about the baby. I mean, I wasn't counting on that."

"You're not saying that because I'm a woman and you want ..."

"No. I got this."

"You got this?" I asked.

"Absolutely, I got this. If you want to help, you can. I think ... Joe will help everyone, but I plan on hogging him and taking the reins myself."

"Not that I don't find it extremely noble, but do you know enough about babies? I didn't think you had children."

He looked at me gently biting his bottom lip before raising his eyes to the sky. Almost as if getting courage to speak. "I didn't. I read every book there was old and new. You wouldn't believe how the rules changed. I even went to classes. I was bound and determined to be a good father." He paused. "I would have been. I really would have. Then the fever came. Wait ..." He reached into his back pocket and pulled out his wallet. After opening it, he lifted a small square and handed it to me. "My son."

I felt the ache when I looked at the ultrasound picture.

"Of course, he was twenty-two weeks there. He made it to thirty-six when Lisa passed away from the fever. She was one of the first in DC to be infected. She took our cat to the vet. They tried to save the baby, but he died, too." He took back the picture and put it in his wallet.

"Brad, I'm sorry."

"That's ..."

"No, listen to me. I am really sorry. I didn't know. I'm sorry for your losses and for being so self-absorbed that I never asked. That was wrong."

"It's okay. You lost your children."

"And you lost your son."

He nodded and replaced his wallet. "I didn't know if I wanted to live. I had the gun right here." He pointed to his temple. "Ready. I mean, I lost Lisa. I lost my son. I was immune. Who wants to live like that? I was ready to pull the trigger when I thought, if I die, then any inkling of my family dies, too. The only way to keep them alive somehow is to keep living and talking ... and showing sonogram pictures.

That's what I do and will always do. So can you see why I want to focus on Joe."

"I can."

"I'm thinking of heading down to that monastery. Even before the fever they grew their own food. They have a doctor there. It might be for the best. You should think about it."

"I will."

"Right now, we need to think about cleaning this town. Let's go get those gas cans."

I was out of words, I didn't know what to say. I spent so much time not liking Brad, I never bothered to find out who he really was. I based my judgment on his attitude. Throwing himself into helping the town, yet I never bothered to think of why. I assumed his motivation was selfishness, it didn't cross my mind it was grief. All the years he and I crossed paths and I still didn't know him, but I knew him a little better and realized he was in no different position than me. He was dealing with the complete loss of his family, as well. He was just handling it differently.

<><><><>

It wasn't as easy as it seemed, or appeared in movies. There was more to burning the dead than just lighting the flame.

It didn't matter how many were in the pile, I still saw the faces of those I know. Pale, wide eyes, decomposing.

Sam had taken Joe to Janice's house, which was on top of the slope and a good distance from the smoke. We all envisioned flames shooting in the air, black smoke and a horrendous stench. The stench was there, but it was smoldering. The bodies didn't immediately catch fire. In their decomposing state they were damp. The putrid smell of burning, rotting flesh and hair filled the air and to make matters worse, the fire kept going out. I wished we had found a huge patch of land, dug a hole and put the bodies there. But it was too late. Every time we had to douse the bodies with gasoline and relight the fire, I felt we were desecrating those in our town. Somehow making them suffer, even though I knew they couldn't feel it.

The piles of bodies never burned to ashes, they just turned to mounds of charred corpses.

We failed because we believed that cleaning up Mills Run would be as simple as lighting a match. That wasn't the case. It was far ahead of us and more than three people alone could handle.

Truth was, the only way to clear all of Mills Run of the bodies was to bury them, or wait until they turned to dust.

It was a long day.

One barge, three mounds and they all still remained.

I walked to Janice's house and cleaned up. Both Sam and Brad were consumed with Joe. I planned to get to know the infant as well. In fact, I had a bin of baby clothes in my father's attic. Brad was right, Joe was good for all of us. Even though I hadn't held him since we pulled him from the pile, he inspired me, without thought, to walk into my home.

However, the moment I stepped inside, I started thinking.

The report cards on the fridge, brought the thought of my children forefront. The wine on the counter made me think of my mother and the keys to the ferry had me not only thinking of my father, but thinking about life.

As much as I wanted it to, the house wasn't full of life, it was just full of memories.

For some reason, I forgot about the baby clothes, grabbed the keys to the ferry, the jug of homemade wine, and Ivy's ashes and I left, without saying anything, and went to the river.

The ferry ... the John Ashton Ferry, that was life.

My father put his heart and soul into that ferry. When times were tough and money was short, that was our vacation home. I loved that ferry nearly as much as my father.

I loved what he had done with it and I adored the fact that he sounded off the foghorn to let me know he was home.

It had been weeks, but I fired up the engines and turned on all the lights.

The main room of the ferry was filled with boxes of food and water. I knew there was even more stowed below. All the supplies my father and I had gathered. The ferry was my father's life and he was going to use it so we kept ours. That was his plan.

I avoided my house because I was afraid of the memories. The memories and feelings weren't in the house, they were on the ferry. I could sense my father, smell him.

In the wheelhouse, I ran my hands over the controls and wheel, then I sounded off the horn. It made me laugh. It sounded so loud. I played the music my father played whenever he made any long trips, then I made my way below, sat on the deck, drinking wine and looking out to the river.

When I closed my eyes, I could hear my father's voice.

"Tie the line, Clare, let's just dock here."

I could hear Michael asking if he could drive the boat and my father yelling at Eli and Ivy to stay away from the railing.

More than I realized, my life was not in Mills Run, it was on that ferry.

"Permission to come aboard?" Sam asked.

I was so lost in my world, I lost track of time. I turned around. Sam and Brad stood there, Brad held the baby.

"Of course," I said.

"We thought you were leaving," Sam said, stepping onto the deck.

"No. I don't even know what possessed me to come down here," I replied.

"It's peaceful and beautiful," Brad said, looking out to the river.

"Could you step away from the railing with the baby," I suggested. "Please."

Brad stepped back.

"What's going on?" Sam asked. "You went to get baby clothes and never came back."

"I went into the house," I said. "It was a rough day. We sucked at burning bodies. My mind was just spinning, but when I walked in the house and saw the ferry keys, I just came here."

"Yes, you did suck," Sam replied. "There's no instruction booklet. You okay?"

"Yeah, yeah, I am. I've been thinking. Mills Run will never be the same. Not yet, not for years. I said I didn't want to leave because my family is here. That's not true. My family is here." I pointed around. "Right here on this boat. Brad, you asked me today about long term survival. What about midterm?"

Sam chuckled. "What are you talking about?"

"My father packed this boat for short term survival. Brad wants to plan on long term. No one plans on the interim. Would you mind not going to the monastery just yet?" I asked Brad. "You're going there to look for life. For a community. We can do that. Us four are life. We can search for more."

"Interim." Brad said. "Meaning, see what's out there before we make long term decisions."

"Exactly. Take my father's plan one step further. We have over twelve hundred river miles. Hundreds of river towns. Let's finish here, get supplies, take the ferry and just go. Find survivors, stop at each town, search out communities. Hell, make our own community. There's no rule or law that says home has to be on land."

"You know." Sam stepped toward me. "We tried to talk to you about this. Take the boat and go."

"I guess I needed it to be my idea." I lowered my head.

"I'm in," Brad said. "Joe's in, too."

I walked over and held out my hands for the baby. "May I?"

"Sure." Brad placed him in my arms.

I cradled him in my arms. Joe was so tiny and precious. He didn't ask to be born into a devastated world. He fought to live and was given a second chance. He deserved a shot at life. The best life we could give him. One filled with promise and hope, not a town filled with decaying bodies.

Where there was water, there was life.

I wasn't sure what all was out there, but I was positive life on the ferry would be better than staying in Mills Run.

I didn't know where my plan would take us, or if it would be successful, but we would take it one day at a time. Like the ferry on the river, we would go with the flow.

THRITY-NINE – BEYOND

July 12

We paid our homage and honor to Mills Run, by taking the time to clear the houses and bury the dead as best as we could. It took four weeks to do so. We used that time so Joe could be at full strength and to gather more supplies, taking from homes and stores. He was doing great and by what we estimated, we had enough to ration for at least four months. That supply amount grew every mile we moved through the river.

Brad rarely left Joe's side, but he did leave town for three days to search out the monastery in Wayne, West Virginia. It was real and everything Brad had heard was true. It was a self-sufficient community of over a hundred people, all behind a huge wall.

He met the leader of the community, a monk named Jeremiah. He encouraged Brad to get us and come live at the monastery. Brad thanked him and said that it was a possibility, perhaps later.

We needed to know if the safe haven monastery was real. It wasn't our goal, going there was an option. A back up scenario in case we didn't succeed.

Yet, we weren't sure what we were even trying to accomplish.

In reality, we didn't have a firm goal.

We were more like locusts. We'd stop, get what we needed and move on. To where was undetermined.

Our journey down the river was slow. We inched our way, stopped when the sun went down, and moved in the morning. Each town we passed, we paused and sounded the horn. We'd leave the ferry and get what we could from the town, then move on.

A lot of times, with supplies, we found people.

In the first two weeks, close to two dozen men and seven children, all boys, boarded the ferry. There was life out there and we were finding it.

Though I bid farewell to my house and family, they weren't far. My room on the ferry was a shrine to my entire life. Pictures graced the walls, trophies, books and Ivy's ashes. I missed them terribly, and I supposed I forever would.

The hole in my heart would never close. Every day it ached for them.

We started a routine. Each night, after supper, we'd sit around telling stories of our families. It started with me, Sam and Brad, but the routine continued even as our numbers grew. It was just more stories to enjoy and absorb.

Brad once said that living was the only way to keep his family alive. He was right. I may had lost my entire family, but I was doing my best by talking about them, showing pictures and keeping their essence alive. In doing so, in a way I was living again, and them through me.

I didn't know when we'd stop and dock for good. We stopped monitoring the radio, looking for civilization because every day we grew in numbers and were our own civilization. We took it one day at a time. The midterm plan was turning into a long term journey and it was working out.

Eventually we'd run out of river. I didn't think that would stop us, not with a sea to conquer as well. We weren't putting time tables or labels on anything.

We were just trying to move on, to survive and with each passing day, we were doing just that.

◇◇◇◇

Thank you so much for reading this book. I hope you enjoyed it. There may be questions you have, by all means send them my way.

Please visit my website www.jacquelinedruga.com and sign up for my mailing list for updates, freebies, new releases and giveaways. And, don't forget my new Kindle club!

Your support is invaluable to me. I welcome and respond to your feedback. Please feel free to email me at Jacqueline@jacquelinedruga.com